Just Like Me
Fallen Victims of the Mind

Just Like Me
Fallen Victims of the Mind

Just Like Me
Fallen Victims of the Mind

Just Like Me
Fallen Victims of the Mind

Just Like Me
Fallen Victims of the Mind

Just Like Me
Fallen Victims of the Mind

Just Like Me
Fallen Victims of the Mind

~ Lena Ma

Copyright ©2020

Just Like Me
Fallen Victims of the Mind

Any references to historical events, real people, or real places are used fictitiously. Names, characters, and places are products of the author's imagination.

Cover Design by Lily Dormishev

Table of Contents

Just Like Me
Fallen Victims of the Mind

Just Like Me
Fallen Victims of the Mind

Prologue

The human mind is extremely malleable, capable of constantly changing ideas and beliefs based on current wants and desires, driven by emotions and vain.

We think we know what we want at any given time. We tell ourselves that we are strong and capable enough to stand by our beliefs and moral concepts, but most of us only do it for show. When opportunity comes up for us to disregard those "core beliefs," we allow it to happen.

As vulnerable human beings, we always believe that the "thing" we do not have is the "thing" that will make our lives complete and our satisfactions whole. We constantly chase after these "things" that others seem to have and automatically correlate them with life happiness.

However, what we continuously fail to realize is that our individual beings are what gives us the most satisfaction, long term that is.

What happens when we can finally afford that new purse that everyone swears "makes their life complete"? What happens when we finally get our hands on that new phone that everyone promises will "provide life-long happiness"?

What happens when we finally reach one million followers on Instagram and receive as many as 5,000 likes and comments per day? Will that give us satisfaction that lies beyond skin-deep? What happens when we finally wake up one morning with the face and body of a model or a celebrity? Will that give us happiness and self-approval that is not only reflected in a mirror?

Think about it. We spend all this time and energy WISHING we could be like someone else, WISHING we have the "things" that others have, and BELIEVING that our lives would be ten times better than they are now if we can just obtain those "things."

These "things," however, are only distractions from a greater issue, a greater issue that lies beneath us, where we obliviously believe that true bliss and fulfillment within ourselves can come from obtaining external objects and replacing the appearance of who we are with the appearance of someone else.

But how can we replace something that's internal with external materials? How can we create inner contentment with external substances? If we obtain that "thing" we crave for so much, won't another "thing" come along at another point in time and make us yearn for that new "thing"?

What if we had the face of the supermodel we are currently envious of? Won't a new supermodel, with a different face, come along and make us wish we could look like the latter?

Transient materials can never provide us with true gratification if we don't know what we are looking for. We never take the time to reflect on what makes us who we are, constantly trying to replace who we are before giving us a chance to figure it out.

We relentlessly believe that we will never have enough or that we will never be good enough because we don't have set goals or expectations. Our beliefs are always changing, based on feelings, based on societal pressure, or based on the need to belong.

We believe that having a different face and appearance will make us more likeable, and therefore, more content with ourselves when we are isolated from partners and social groups. However, this strong desire fades when we feel welcomed and accepted by those we crave acceptance from.

We believe that gaining fame through social media and becoming a well-known influencer will drive greater gratification in us toward life when those around us criticize us as being "no one" or "nothing" otherwise.

We believe that if everyone around us likes us then, eventually, we will learn to like ourselves. However, without this pressure driving us toward reaching fame and glory, our thoughts and desires may be completely different.

We believe that obtaining that new phone or that new purse will make us feel like we belong in certain social groups because society has told us that certain social groups are the "best ones," and if we are not in them, we do not have value.

Even if we have previously opposed or loathed the "popular" social groups, we give into the pressure when we feel we are being left out.

The constant need to be what everyone else is or to have what everyone else has only makes us miss out on the qualities that make us human.

The endless mission we have in searching for what we don't have only causes us to miss out on what we do have, eventually triggering us to completely forget why we even began that mission, leaving us to blindly follow what we no longer understand.

Chapter One

The wind blows. The crows caw. The rain pours.

One sits on a wooden bench, secluded in the middle of a dark forest underneath the gloomy clouds, gazing deeply into Two's eyes.

It is the year 2065 and the forest is desolate, but the sounds of the blaring city of Lustville can still be heard from a distance. The forest is adorned with web-covered tombstones, scattered chaotically throughout the land, and non-flowering green bushes, sprawled across the perimeter of the woods.

There are a couple of abandoned trucks and cars for sexually-charged teens and adulterers, along with a few half-buried bodies lying beneath the soil, but other than that, the forest is mostly covered with dead grass and crumbling rocks.

It is a frigid winter afternoon, with a thunderstorm brewing behind the threatening clouds, embracing the entire town in its pertinent darkness. One's silver white hair covers his head, with his bangs hanging over the left side of his face, hiding his expression of indifference.

Two sits, submissively, across from him, with her long curly silver white hair flowing in the strong wind, gusting locks of hair across her perfectly oval face, embellished with dark brown eyes and thin painted lips.

Two stares back at One, seemingly timid and shy, and smiles.

"Two." One says, holding onto her small hands. "I think we should get married."

Two shifts, uncomfortably, while adjusting her long silver dress.

"I think so too." Two replies. "But what about your relationship with Three?"

"That can still continue. Three is aware of my relationship with you. Besides, I'll get tired of her soon enough anyway. You can also have your own side relationship. I've been waiting for you to get one."

"Hmm, well I do have Four. But, won't Three have a problem with you marrying me? Don't you want her more?"

"Why would she have a problem? She knows she's nothing more to me than an affair. Besides, she would never leave her husband for me. You and I have better chemistry than me and her, or even you and Four. You know that."

"I suppose you're right. Okay, I'll marry you!"

As soon as Two finishes her sentence, One reaches into his pocket, pulling out a small and red velvet box. He opens it, revealing the most stunning ring embedded in amethyst lining. The ring has a diamond stone, shining magnificently even in the midst of gloomy dusk.

One slips it onto Two's already held out ring finger, over the tan line of her previous ring, and they kiss. They are now engaged to be married.

Watching this, through binoculars, from a latticed apartment window facing the forest, is Five. Five's modern apartment building complex is sixteen stories high, overlooking the town of Lustville and painted a beautiful hue of silver.

Standing inside her twelfth-floor apartment, she peers out into the woods with a blank expression on her face.

Her living room is decorated with silver antique pieces of furniture she bought from multiple thrift stores. There are two old-fashioned light silver velvet armchairs in the middle of the room.

Five's oldest friend sits on one of the chairs, sipping a cup of pumpkin spice latte and crunching on kale chips.

She looks like Five, with neatly curled long silver white hair hanging loosely down her back and a single strand of her bangs decorating her structured face. Five is wearing a long and flowing silver dress while her friend is wearing the same.

After staring absent-mindedly and indifferently at both Two and One for over an hour, Five walks away from the window, staring at the ring on her finger and running her thumb over an engraving that says, "One Loves Five Forever," without a single emotion drawn on her face.

She cannot remember why this ring is on her finger. She cannot recall whether this ring means something or who One is, for that matter. She only assumes that this ring is one of the many she had stolen from her friends over the years.

She sits back down, placing herself gently on the light silver armchair across from her friend.

"Well, Six, it's been a while since we saw each other. What do you want?" Five interrogates, calmly.

"No reason. I was just in the neighborhood and wanted to stop by to see my good friend."

Her friend, Six, replies, taking another sip of her pumpkin spice latte.

"Six, we haven't seen or spoken to each other in years. I barely recognized you when you rang my doorbell. Now, tell me, why are you here?"

"Alright, fine, fine. You caught me. I just need to borrow some money. I've been struggling to make ends meet since my husband passed away. The little I get from the government is barely enough to cover my basic expenses like food and rent."

Six grins, wickedly, as Five turns around to pick up her cup of pumpkin spice latte.

"Well, MY HUSBAND is extremely wealthy, bringing in more money than we could ever spend. We are, in fact, on our way to becoming millionaires. Of course, I can spare you some chump change." Five laughs, boastfully.

With this, she gets up from her seat and walks off, with perfect and petite steps, into her bedroom. Barely a minute later, she returns with a wad of cash in her hand.

"Here you go. Two thousand dollars. That should be more than enough. Now get out of here, you filthy hobo." Five says, tossing the money at Six, bills scattering across her silver carpet.

Six beams at Five as she gets down on her knees to pick up the money.

"Thank you, Five. Thank you! I owe you one. You're the best!" Six replies, picking her small silver purse up from the floor as she stands up and walks out the front door.

Back in her own apartment, the most expensive luxury condominium in the city, Six walks into her bedroom, painted royal silver with gold embellishments, and tosses her cheap and old purse into a hamper labeled "Props."

On one side of her room stands a tall shelf, lined with numerous name-brand and luxury purses. She lightly touches one adorned with gold diamonds and chuckles to herself.

"I can't believe that idiot was stupid enough to buy my story. No wonder we're no longer friends." Six laughs, roguishly, as she surrounds herself with thousands of purses she had bought with the money she got from scamming people.

Chapter Two

The city trembles as the towering bell rings. Work has ended, and the streets become packed with hordes of men rushing into their silver cars and speeding to get home, disregarding the dozens of deaths and accidents they cause every day in the process.

Men dressed in silver dress shirts and silver tailored pants line the streets as they cross each other with simultaneous steps and huge grins decorating their faces. The men all smile at each other, saying "hello," with obvious fallacy, as if they are on auto-pilot.

Seven stands in front of his work building. Seven is a small fellow, with a balding silver white hairline and brown eyes. Seven has just been laid off from his job for shooting the CEO of his company, smiling and grinning despite the horrible situation.

He scans the crowd around him for his prey, watching men robotically walk by him, one by one. Out of the corner of his eye, he sees a tall and thin man, dressed in a silver dress shirt and silver tailored pants, cross the street.

Seven had stolen from others in the past, during the many other times he had lost his job, and because he is far from being a professional, his method of action is usually to resort to physical violence.

Seven is small and stout, but violence and physical blows come naturally to him. He has been training, learning to fight and wrestle, for the past five years.

Confidently, Seven comes up behind the man, grabs him by the collar, and yanks the man to the ground. The man falls, taken aback by the sudden attack. People surrounding them begin to form a crowd, entertaining themselves by cheering and betting money on who will be victorious.

Seven has full control over the man, driving a wrenching punch into the man's abdomen. The man doubles over in pain, waving his hands up as a sign of forfeiture, allowing Seven to steal his wallet, his keys, and his car.

The crowd around them continues to cheer and clap for Seven, without noticing or caring that they had just witnessed assault and theft. Seven slowly drives away, unaware and unconcerned that the man he had just fought is bleeding to his death.

Watching this scene unfold, in the luxury of her sleek silver car, parked along the sidewalk in front of a regal jewelry store called "The Glam," is Eight.

Eight had been traveling around the world for the past six months, shopping in cities like Milaxa and Pasira, and lying on beaches in islands like the Malvyves and

Seychyllix. She stopped when she heard the commotion on her way back home.

She had watched the fight with indifference. Like all the others, she does not see a problem in what had happened. She sees fights like this almost every day as part of her normal routine, almost as if she is watching television.

Glancing around the streets, Eight notices a few local bookstores advertising her latest book, "Be Your Best You," a self-help and psychological novel teaching young women how to channel their own unique personalities, accept their flaws, and become aware of their own moral conscience.

Eight feels proud of herself as she sees a group of young women, all dressed in long silver dresses, gawking at her book through the store windows.

Everybody in town knows Eight. She is a local celebrity. She cannot remember her life prior to becoming famous five years ago, prior to having one of her social media posts on a popular platform called "BLykeMe," where she stands at a rally protesting about how women deserve be different and independent, along with hundreds of other women dressed in long silver dresses, go viral, and propel her into fame.

Everyone in town loves posting about their life on BLykeMe, as it is the only social media platform that allows people to share openly and honestly without consequences or judgments.

Women in Lustville do not have professional careers. They thrive on their husbands taking care of them and giving them the money they want to buy themselves expensive presents and gifts.

Lustville is no ordinary town. In Lustville, individual differences do not exist. Everyone is the same. Everyone looks the same.

Everyone dresses the same. Everyone behaves the same. Everyone is a clone of the person sitting or standing next to him or her. In this town, unique thoughts and unique opinions do not exist. Personalities do not exist. No one is able to explain their own identities because no one has an identity.

There are no names, no individual minds, no souls. However, because of this, no one is able to fault another person for their sins. No one is able to generate feelings of anger or envy toward another because there are no longer reasons to.

No one is able to generate emotions at all, only mimicking gestures that they have been taught and programmed to have, with no true understanding of why they are creating such gestures.

Everyone is free to do whatever they want, no consequences, no blame, no morals. Everyone is a branch off the same dysfunctional tree.

Chapter Three

"RING!" The cacophonous alarm sounds, alarming the songbirds as they fly off the windowsill of Fourteen's apartment and into the fierce wind.

It is a cold winter morning, with the bright sun shining behind the thick overcast clouds. Rain had slowly been trickling down from the dark sky for the past seven hours.

Startled, Fourteen jumps up from her soft bed, covered with silver decorated pillows and silver polyester sheets. She had just been dreaming about her sweet and sane life back home, where people are different yet proud of it.

Instead, she wakes up to the soulless life she is living now, a life on auto-pilot, unable to do or say as she pleases or else she risks getting killed.

Fourteen is not a morning person, as she yawns and wipes the drool off her chin. Her alarm had surprised her so much that she almost fell out of bed, which she had done once or twice, or ten times, before. She opens her eyes to an eerily quiet morning, as she usually does.

She does not know how she can predict it, but eerily quiet mornings are usually a warning that someone is about to die. Back home, this used to surprise people. People used to come from all over the world and awe at her premonitions. Some even feared her as they thought being closer to her meant a higher chance of dying.

However, in Lustville, where death happens so often, no one seems to care about her premonitions. Every quiet morning for her is met with fear and anxiety, with full knowledge that death is going to surround her and there is nothing she can do about it.

She shakes her head to get the fear out of her mind. There is never enough time in the mornings to worry about anything as she must present herself to her husband under gift wrap and bow (not literally, of course).

She hears the water running in the shower.

"Nine must be getting ready for work. I need to hurry!" Fourteen exclaims, as she quickly climbs out of bed and runs over to her vanity.

Her old vanity was decorated with photos of her travel experiences and the fun times she had with her friends back home. This new vanity, however, must remain a plain silver color so Fourteen would not accidentally get emotional over looking at a picture of her old life, especially in front of her husband.

Since only programmed emotions are allowed in Lustville, Fourteen has to carefully select the emotions she portrays in public. Whenever she feels an emotion that is "not programmed," she forces herself to wear a mask just to cover up her face.

Experiencing emotions that are not part of protocol causes the chip to beep, and since she doesn't have a chip, Fourteen must take caution to avoid getting caught and hung over the infamous bridge of Lustville, where all the bodies of "sinners" remain for eternity.

At her vanity, Fourteen rummages through boxes upon boxes of makeup that her husband had bought for her over the past few months. She normally doesn't wear makeup but, again, dressing up faces like clowns is one of the requirements of this world.

She grabs some powder and mascara, and she slaps them on her face to pretty herself up. There is a certain look that women in Lustville must wear. Eyelashes must be dark and thick. Eyebrows must be full and silver white. Lipstick must be adorned with a gentle brush of gloss.

Eyeliner and eyeshadow must always be different shades of black, and contouring is a must. Fourteen never even knew what contouring was before coming to Lustville.

"What's the point of creating fake lines on your body? It's barbaric! You either have it or you don't!" She quietly mumbles to herself every morning as she covers her face like a clown queen and pops a stick of gum into her mouth.

Gum. That's another thing. Gum is not allowed in Lustville because it has the potential of getting caught in someone's hair and ruining it. Anything that can accidentally ruin the appearance of Lustville and cause people to look different from one another is banned.

Fourteen is addicted to gum. She chews it whenever she gets nervous, and in a world where she must pretend to be someone she despises every second of the day, chewing gum seems to be the only thing keeping her sane.

Before she left, she had stashed her suitcase with packs and packs of gum. Luckily, the security in Lustville cared more about what was in Fourteen's head than what was in her luggage.

Despite not seeing any use in adorning her face to look like a Halloween mask, she continues to every morning despite her opposing thoughts. Nine is not allowed to see her without a face of makeup on.

It is an unwritten rule that she must look "her best" for Nine whenever he sees her. She is only allowed to sleep after he sleeps so she could wash her makeup off, and she must sleep facing the opposite direction of Nine so he doesn't see her "disturbing" face in the mornings.

Thirty minutes of struggling with a blush brush and concealer later, she hurries into her closet, pulls out her long silver dress from the day before, hoping it doesn't smell as she had forgotten to do laundry, and draws it over her head, brushing it off as it flows to the ground.

Every morning is the same. Every morning needs to be the same. Every morning, Fourteen must be ready, perfectly pressed and groomed by the time Nine steps out of the shower.

She hears the shower turn off as the water drips.

"Shit!" Fourteen whispers to herself, bolting out of her closet.

Nine spends exactly eighteen minutes in the bathroom every morning after he turns the shower off. However, Fourteen must be ready and prepared the minute he turns the water off if he ever decides to step out earlier.

Seven minutes go by, and Nine is still in the bathroom. Fourteen can hear him still drying off his silver white locks. Nine loves to admire himself in the mirror whenever he steps foot into the bathroom, flexing his biceps and gleaming at his pecks and rock-hard abs.

"Shit!" Fourteen whispers to herself again, as she realizes that she is still chewing her gum.

She spits it out onto her left palm and reaches under her dress to hide it. She makes sure to secure her gum inside her underwear so it doesn't accidentally slip out in front of

Nine. Nine has a zero-tolerance policy when it comes to chewing gum. If he ever caught her doing so, he would have no problem shooting her on the spot.

Last month, Nine found a gum wrapper in Fourteen's purse while he was looking for a pencil. Pencils are the only writing tools allowed in Lustville as pencil marks can be erased, making the canvas clean again without any unneeded permanent damage.

Fourteen likes to associate the erasing attribute of pencils with the clean slate in Lustville. No one has memories. No one has imperfections. No one has lives.

Nine almost beat Fourteen to death after he found the wrapper in her purse, only sparing her after she thoroughly explained to him that she bought the wrapper from a store called "The Other World" because she was curious as to what they looked like. She swore to him that she had no idea what and how gum even tastes like!

Even so, even if Nine does pound her to death, it would not matter as no one would care. Everyone in town would just praise Nine for his blunt strength and tenacity.

Eighteen minutes on the dot, Nine finally comes out of the bathroom, the bathroom filling up with steam and a strong scent of cologne behind him. He walks straight pass Fourteen without acknowledging her or even looking her way, leaving Fourteen standing there, smiling obnoxiously without breaking character.

This is no surprise. Nine never looks toward her way in the mornings. Ever since he "claimed" her, his interest in her has dwindled more and more. He spends more time with other women, constantly bringing them home while ignoring Fourteen.

However, Fourteen continues to dress up in her "daily routine" because if she does not look picture perfect for her husband, consequences would be dire. She does not know what the consequences would be, but she doesn't want to find out.

In fact, Nine rarely ever speaks to Fourteen. They are married, but they do not love each other. How could they when love in Lustville is nonexistent? Before moving to Lustville, Fourteen had a fiancé, named Elijah, whom she loved. They were together for over ten years and spent every moment of every day together.

Sadly, five years ago, he committed suicide when his application for the "Hot & Young Fashion Influencer Program" was rejected, and the program selected men who were much brooder and richer than him.

Becoming a fashion influencer had always been Elijah's dream. They did not have a lot of money, so he had created his entire collection and style based on thrift store clothing and charitable donations. His social media page was extremely popular among the lower class, but the upper class always had the final say in who became the next "big thing."

After his death, Fourteen became extremely depressed and wanted to run away. She could no longer handle living inside her home, surrounded by constant reminders that her fiancé is no longer alive. She knew about the development of the chip and Lustville.

She saw it as the perfect chance to escape reality and live a fresh life on a blank slate. She hastily threw some of her belongings inside her suitcase, bracing herself for the new lifestyle she was about to endure, and hopped on the last plane flying out to Lustville.

However, what she didn't realize back then, is that life in Lustville is far different than the life she had envisioned, far worse than the life she had lived back home.

Upon arrival, she was screened and given a set of questions to ensure that she was indeed "one of them" and that she would not rebel. Everyone who enters Lustville is required to have a chip inside their brain and answer "yes" to every question asked.

Fourteen does not have the chip in her brain, but she was able to get past security because she had helped develop the chip and knew how to get around the requirements of entering the "new world."

On her second day in Lustville, Fourteen met Nine while walking across the streets after struggling for over an hour getting into her new "uniform."

Nine is a tall brooding man who wanted her and refused to take "no" for an answer. He continued to pester and follow her until she agreed to sleep with him, engaging in matrimony with him a few short months later.

Attempting to blend in with the common crowd in her new society, Fourteen agreed to marry Nine, despite how much she found Nine repulsive and still missed Elijah. It is much easier to pretend like she belongs in Lustville when she agrees, so her strong and forceful opinions would not accidentally shine through and give her away.

After Nine leaves their apartment for work, Fourteen quickly erases the dumb smile off her face, takes her gum out of her underwear, and hides it in her suitcase with hundreds of her other chewed up gum. She cannot risk flushing the wads of gum down the toilet as she may become exposed if they clog the sewer pipes.

There is not a lot to do in Lustville. Men often went to work, raped heavily, or murdered those who stood in their ways, while women often spent their mornings posting selfies on social media, their afternoons spending thousands of dollars on useless trinkets, and their evenings cheating on their partners.

However, there is a rule, another one of those unspoken ones in Lustville. Each and every woman in town must purchase at least six new items every day as a way to prove that they belong in this world.

Otherwise, their chips would begin to beep as a sign of difference, and they would immediately shatter. The women in Lustville generally have no issues when it comes to abiding by this rule. They are in this world for a reason. They were brought here because they no longer wanted to have their own voices and wanted the chance to have what everyone else has.

Many nights, Fourteen dreams about going back home, her real home. She wishes she had known about the nightmare Lustville was capable of becoming before she decided to sneak in. However, she is not allowed to leave this world as long as the Lustville people still exist.

People who enter Lustville are stuck in Lustville. They are forbidden to have any contact with the other world to avoid contaminating the "normies." They craved a mindless world where they are able to do and have all that they want, and they got that world.

There is no turning back.

Unless. Unless Fourteen can find a way to stop the chip and turn everyone in town back to normal. Only then, would the other world allow them to return back to their original lives.

Although Fourteen took part in the research and the creation of the chip, she does not possess all the knowledge of the chip. Her best friend and colleague, Charlotte Densen, is the main creator and the people of Lustville's, and her, only chance of living a normal life again.

However, Charlotte had also been infected by the chip, and she had turned from a prestigious neuroscientist to a ditzy influencer and adulterer.

"Here we go again. Another day of useless, mindless shopping for shit I just chuck inside my closet." Fourteen grunts to herself, as she squeezes her feet into her tight black platform shoes and leaves her apartment to do her daily shopping.

Fourteen is not a materialistic person. Not at all. She hates the idea of using objects in attempts to replace true happiness and self-satisfaction. She has no problem with other people being consumed by materialism, but Fourteen would rather spend her time and money on adventures and travels, experiences that could not be replaced, moments she could cherish forever.

Swinging her $8,000 Prada handbag and throwing on a fake smile, Fourteen joins the rest of the women in Lustville, also swinging handbags and fake smiling, on the streets. They are all dressed in long silver dresses while wearing black platform shoes, and they all say "hello" to people they walk past even though they don't truly mean it.

'This is like a freaking horror movie. Everyone is a damn clone!' Fourteen thinks to herself.

Because she does not technically have the chip inside her brain, any opinionated thoughts she has that contradict popular beliefs would not trigger her demise and cause her to shatter. She only needs to remember to keep her thoughts inside her mind and not expose them to the public. The chip cannot destroy her, but the people sure can.

After saying "hello" to about 150 different people and trying not to break character, Fourteen finds herself standing in front of The Glam, the most obnoxiously decked out building Fourteen has ever seen, with people literally dressed in sterling silver as they walk out of it, and she goes in.

'I want to puke.' Fourteen thinks to herself as she comes face to face with the highly decorated interior of the building, completely filled with wide-eyed soulless creatures greedily destroying each other for the tiniest of rings.

'Alright, let's just get this over with.'

Fourteen steps onto the lush silver velvet rug and finds herself surrounded by dozens upon dozens of chandeliers and candelabras. Every wall and every crevice of the building are adorned with metallic silver and gold embellishments, as the reflections from the glaring sun blind her wherever she turns.

Just Like Me
Fallen Victims of the Mind

After sixty brutal minutes of aimlessly wandering around and PRETENDING to adore all the items in the store (sixty minutes is the minimum amount of time women in Lustville are allowed to "window shop"), she stops by one seemingly empty counter, calls the salesman over, who looks like he had just stepped out of a hair gel factory, and she randomly picks out the first six jewelry pieces from around the store that she can see, with zero care as to what they look like and trying hard to not fall asleep as the salesman describes, in excruciating detail, that the pieces she had picked out also comes in a variety of stones and colors.

"You look like an amethyst girl. How about I go into the back and get you some gorgeous cuts of amethyst and emerald to go with your dazzling eyes?" The salesman continues.

"Thanks, but I think these pieces would do just fine." Fourteen replies.

"Oh, stop being so humble! You deserve the best! Now, how about you just wait right here, and I'll go fetch them for you!" He insists, as he flies off like a fairy toward the back of the store.

A few minutes later, he dances back with a large tray, covered in a variety of different stones.

"And here we have…"

"I'll take them all!" Fourteen exclaims, interrupting the salesman as she hands over her credit card.

She does not have the patience for him to describe all 73 stones on that tray. She just wants to get the hell out of that bedazzled store. Besides, it's not like she's spending her own money anyway.

"Alrighty, then! Let me just go package these up for the beautiful queen."

Fourteen watches as the salesman prances off to the register.

Out of the corner of her eye, she notices a group of young women lashing insults out at one another, calling each other "slut" and "whore," over one little bracelet. Some women in Lustville like to engage in competitions. In this one, "The Whore-Off" as Fourteen likes to call it, whichever woman can make the rest of the group trigger their sadness emotion first, wins.

Minutes later, the salesman comes prancing back with her credit card and roughly 30 little shopping bags, his silver pressed suit shining brightly beneath the sun roof. Fourteen takes them from his hands, leans in so he can snap a selfie of the two of them together (taking selfies has become the new version of saying "thank you"), and leaves the store, dreading having to repeat this nightmare the next day.

Chapter Four

Eight rolls back onto her side of the bed, completely naked, relaxed, and satisfied. The strapping man beside her gets up almost immediately and walks into her silver-tiled bathroom. Eight admires Nine's magnificent figure from afar.

He is extremely tall and broad-shouldered, with washboard abs that define his body. He has silver white curls that reach up to his ears, dark eyes hidden behind long black lashes, and the most perfect jawline decorated by the slightest hint of a silver stubble.

As pleasing as he is to the eyes, Nine is even more pleasing in bed. Eight smiles as she reflects on the intense and passionate love they had just shared moments ago. Nine had caressed her and kissed her in all the right places, and had made Eight moan numerous times.

Suddenly feeling shy, Eight wraps the silver satin sheets around her naked body and lies back down, watching the ceiling fan whirl continuously in circles.

It is a cold winter afternoon. Eight looks outside her window, through her silver curtains, and sees the snow beginning to flurry down. The sun shines fiercely down onto her apartment complex, and its heat creeps inside Eight's opened bedroom windows, warming her exposed toes from underneath her silver satin sheets.

Eight hears Nine turn on the shower. She knows that he will leave immediately after, as true feelings of intimacy are not common in Lustville. However, Eight does not mind it much, for intimacy is not something she craves. It is an unfamiliar concept to her, and she cannot remember a time when she truly felt in love.

Suddenly, she hears the front door sling open. Nine is still in the shower so it could not have been him leaving. Unalarmed, Eight stands up from her bed and wraps herself in her long silver robe. She slowly tiptoes up to her bedroom door, which is slightly ajar. Through the slit, she peeks into the living room and sees her husband, Ten, standing at the front door.

"EIGHT!" Her husband yells, his voice heavy and loud.

Hearing the loud voice of Eight's husband, Nine re-enters the bedroom from the adjoining bathroom. He has a towel wrapped around his groin, but other than that, he is stark naked. Even at that critical moment, Eight finds herself admiring the way Nine's curls, now damp, falls back from his head. His wet lashes give definition to his dark and beautiful eyes.

However, only after seconds of admiring Nine, Ten slams open the bedroom door, and the two men come face-to-face, with Ten scowling and frowning while Nine smiling and smirking. Eight looks over at both men, and for the first time ever, she feels a sinking feeling in her stomach.

Eight has never been loyal to Ten. In the past three years of their marriage, she has slept with numerous people, men and women included. However, Ten never minded as fidelity is not a concept known to either of them.

In fact, Ten is not loyal to Eight either. She had come home, many times, finding Ten in bed with several different women, neighbors and friends included.

Did they yearn for loyalty? Perhaps. Eight does find herself occasionally wondering about what it would be like to have a faithful partner and to be faithful to a partner in return.

However, such thoughts were always short-lived. Her mind does not allow her to entertain these preposterous feelings; her head always aches and pains whenever these thoughts come into her mind.

However, Nine is different. For Eight, Nine is just another affair. For Ten, however, it is a different issue. Eight knew what she was getting herself into the moment she ripped off Nine's silver dress shirt. After all, Nine is Ten's biggest business rival.

Nonetheless, she continues to admire Nine, caressing his naked body, biting his lips, and sucking on his rock-solid shaft as Ten stares at the two of them together, emotionless and unmoved. Nine pushes Eight off him, gathers his clothes from the floor, dropping his towel and allowing Eight to lick his shaft several more times in front of Ten, before walking out the door, and home to his wife.

Eight feels the sinking feeling in her stomach expand and seep into her heart, and her headache intensifies in response to it. She slowly makes her way into bed and sits down in attempts to compose herself.

Ten walks over and sits down next to her.

"Eight, I've never cared about your affairs. But, why did you have to choose Nine out of all the men you could have had? You know he is my rival." Ten says, calmly.

"Why should I care about your animosity with Nine?" Eight replies, almost immediately and unconcernedly.

As she speaks, she can feel her head throb even more, as if her brain is swelling and pushing against her skull. Is she starting to feel something toward this situation? Is she starting to care about what she had done? Is she starting to feel guilty? What is guilt anyway?

"It's not about caring, Eight. It's about business. You know he could hurt our income, the income that I support this household and your wardrobe with. Well, anyway, what's happened has happened. Now I have a legitimate reason to get rid of him. Now I can abolish him." Ten states, almost too calmly.

Suddenly feeling nauseated, Eight walks into her closet to change. She cannot brush off this bothersome feeling like there is something wrong. She winces as she feels daggers digging into her brain.

Dropping her bathrobe, she pulls a long silver dress over her head and opens it down over her legs. She walks past her husband, who is eating out another woman on their kitchen countertop, and leaves the apartment.

Eight has no idea where she is going. She just felt the need to leave her apartment. She walks off into the streets and sees that everyone and everything around her are picture perfect, smiling like they had just rolled out of a modeling catalog and addressing those around them like greeting cards, with nothing out of place.

Eight has only ever felt this headache once before, right before she became betrothed to Ten, and had questioned whether she should have stabbed the old man who crashed her wedding.

Little did she know, that old man was her father, but she could not recognize him at the time. However, that headache quickly subsided when she stopped questioning the rules of society and whether her thoughts were justified.

That is until now. Eight finds herself experiencing an even more intense headache than she had experienced in the past. The headache has now succeeded the sinking feeling in her stomach. Eight does not know how to get over this feeling. For the first time in five years, Eight feels conflicted.

Eight continues to walk a few blocks down to a nearby forest to calm her thoughts. She climbs up a hill, sits at the peak, and stares off into town.

After pushing her conflicting thoughts aside, her headache quells and the sinking feeling in her stomach disappears. Feeling like herself once again, Eight heads home.

Walking into her apartment, Eight sees her husband's figure sitting on the silver sofa, crouched over his laptop. Nine and Ten could have been twins; they look physically alike. Like Nine, Ten is also extremely tall and broad-shouldered, with defined muscles. He also has silver white curls, but slightly shorter than Nine's.

Eight looks over at the ticking clock and sees that it is almost midnight. She had forgotten about dinner! Hurriedly, she pulls out a pot from the cabinet and boils some water so she could make their nightly dinner meal of plain white rice and boiled chicken.

Cooking is a woman's only job in her town as Eight is not well-versed in anything else. However, despite this, Eight believes it is a fair trade-off for being able to buy anything and everything she wants with her husband's money without having to get a real job.

Ten is aware of Eight's presence but makes no attempt to talk to her. Eight knows that Ten is not bothered by her; there is no reason for him to be. He is completely apathetic to what had happened between her and Nine. If Eight guessed right, Ten's biggest agenda right now is to murder Nine.

Ten always took great pride in his killings. He is a popular murderer, admired for his skills by those around him. For that reason, everybody attempts to always be on Ten's good side.

Eight had married Ten because they are physically compatible. They are deeply and sexually attracted to each other, and the chemistry between them is out of this world. People in Lustville marry each other solely based on sexual attraction. Eight has yet to meet a man who attracts her as much as Ten attracts her, but if she does, she would have no problem moving on.

There are no ties between Eight and Ten that cannot be broken. Their marriage could easily be shattered with the snap of a finger and neither of them would think anything of it.

However, Eight has no immediate plans to leave Ten. Nine might have been attractive and a great lover, but he still does not match up to Ten's regal.

This thought reminds Eight that she has not yet posted about Nine on her social media platforms. She quickly scrolls through the photos in her phone for the selfie she had taken with Nine while they were in bed and posts it on all her socials with #mynewcatch.

Everybody in town knows of the professional animosity between Nine and Ten. Eight is sure that she would be congratulated for her top-notch affair by all her friends. Nonetheless, somehow this knowledge only leaves her feeling uneasy.

Just like how Ten is a lucrative murderer, Eight is a lucrative adulterer. She engages in long and devastating affairs, primarily with married men. Eight also takes great pride in her status as an adulterer. Many wives struggle to have meaningful and enjoyable extramarital affairs.

Eight has never struggled to do so. She almost always has a partner in addition to Ten, who were almost always great lovers and always physically attractive. However, at that moment, Eight begins to question what she is doing, shaking her head to try and dispel each passing thought.

As soon as she finishes cooking, Eight calls Ten over, who swiftly waltzes into the kitchen. He plops himself down on his usual silver kitchen chair while Eight bustles around setting the plates and utensils. Eight watches as Ten stares at the picture she had posted with Nine on BLykeMe. Without even as much as a wince, he moves onto the next picture.

Suddenly, Eight feels the sinking feeling returning, but she distracts herself with other thoughts to prevent the screeching headache from returning.

The silence between Eight and Ten is deafening.

However, Ten soon breaks the silence.

"I have the perfect plan to murder Nine." Ten claims, calm and composed.

"Oh? What is it?" Eight questions, nonchalantly.

"It's a secret." Ten whispers, driving suspense.

He looks content with whatever plan he has concocted. However, Eight could not care less about how Ten plans to kill Nine. In fact, she does not care at all about Nine's potential death. Is she supposed to care?

Later that night, Eight prepares for a good night's rest, hoping to relax her mind and stop her thoughts from reoccurring. After clearing the dishes, Eight gets ready for bed. To her delight, Ten had gone out for the night, probably to sleep with their neighbor next door. Eight has the entire bed and apartment to herself, falling asleep as soon as her head hits the pillows.

Eight wakes up the next morning to find Ten's side of the bed still empty, albeit slept on.

'He must have slipped into bed and left early, only sleeping for a few hours.' Eight thinks to herself.

Feeling refreshed and more like herself again, Eight gets out of bed and jumps into the shower. As she stands under the shower head, with the sharp lines of water pouring down her body, she plans the rest of the day for herself.

Women in Lustville do not have jobs. They stay home and complete domestic chores. Hence, Eight occupies herself with household work for the rest of the day, leaving her apartment only twice, once to buy herself three diamond rings from The Glam, and once to purchase three new pairs of pumps from a local shoe store called "The Heel."

The rest of the week goes by smoothly. Ten had made no further comments about Nine, and Eight had found her life returning to normal as well. She has also begun flirting with a potential new lover, Eleven, an exhibitionist who fornicates with her whenever they step foot out in public.

However, this peace does last long.

Exactly a week later, Eight wakes up one day to find Ten already gone, as usual. Eight had noticed the laundry hamper piling up yesterday, so she decides that she would devote her time today toward laundry. Little does she know, this is not just another ordinary day.

After a quick shower, Eight dresses herself in a long silver dress. As she stands in front of the mirror brushing her hair, Eight finds a tired-looking woman staring back at her. She has silver white hair that falls down to her waist in cascading waves. She looks quite short and has a womanly figure with lush curves and full breasts.

She looks perfectly healthy, except for the presence of slight dark circles under her eyes and the strange electric shocks protruding from the top of her head.

Unconcerned, Eight brushes it off.

After getting ready, Eight walks into the kitchen to make herself some breakfast. Ten usually leaves very early in the morning so Eight mostly eats breakfast by herself. She fixes herself some rice cakes and half a grapefruit, along with a mug of black coffee, and she gulps it all down in barely ten minutes. She then starts the washing machine to get the laundry going and lazily lies down on the sofa, turning on her favorite soap opera.

Snuggling up underneath her soft silver blanket, Eight hears her phone vibrate just as she turns on the television. It is a BLykeMe notification. Thinking that it is just one of her posts getting a verified comment, Eight opens it to find a photo that her husband had tagged her in. The graphic photo shows Ten kneeling down next to a mutilated body, smiling. The body is backside up, so Eight struggles to identify who it was.

This is not unusual for Eight. Ten has a reputation for being an infamous killer, and people in town often boast about their greatest kills. Eight then reads the caption, which says, "Just killed my rival and my wife's special friend."

The sinking feeling returns to Eight's stomach. After a week of peace and quiet, she feels her head beginning to throb again. What is wrong with her? Why does murder bother her suddenly when it never has before?

Eight stares closer at the photo, recognizing the location. It is the front of her apartment building!

Turning off the television, Eight races downstairs and out the front door, finding a group of people gathered around in a circle. In the middle, stands Ten, smiling over Nine's dead body and holding a large and bloody butcher knife in his right hand. The crowd of people all laugh, cheer, and applaud Ten.

Eight would have done the same, as she usually does, but this time is different. This time, all she feels is the queasy, sinking feeling.

Eight can feel her entire body sway with a sensation that pulsates throughout her entire body. Suddenly, she hears a beeping noise inside her head.

She has heard these beeps before, as has everyone, for they are not uncommon. Most people have heard beeping noises in their heads at one point in time, and they all fear the reason as to why.

An ambulance pulls up, and the paramedics slowly load Nine's decapitated body onto a stretcher. There is no attempt to resuscitate him or to punish Ten for his murder. Instead, Ten is lauded as the hero of the whole incident.

Is that not how it is supposed to be?

Eight does not know or understand why, but she begins to question the series of events that had just happened and how it seems immoral, regardless of everyone cheering. She finds her headache progressing further and the sinking feeling enhancing.

By now, she experiences that feeling leave her stomach and enter her bloodstream; she can feel it shake her very body to the core. Eight tries hard to calm herself but nothing seems to help. Her head is still quietly beeping.

Giving up, she walks back into her apartment, lies on her sofa, closes her eyes, and slowly drifts off.

Eight wakes up around midnight again with Ten hovering over her body, still bloody. The uneasy feeling had disappeared, and her head is no longer beeping.

"Dinner." He says, smiling like a child in a chocolate factory.

For a minute, Eight thought that Ten had prepared dinner for the both of them. However, she soon realizes he is only demanding for her to make dinner, now that she is awake. She stands up and rushes to the kitchen, fixing her dress and hair along the way. She quickly sets pots and pans on the stove and begins to boil water.

While preparing dinner, Eight tries to not think about what had happened today, lest her headache returns. Nonetheless, she could not stop thinking about it. Why does murder bother her suddenly? What is that sensation, that sensation that overpowers all her senses, and makes her head beep?

Throwing these unanswered questions aside, she sits down for dinner with Ten.

"What happened to you?" Ten asks, uninterestedly.

"Nothing, I just feel a little sick, that's all." Eight replies, meekly.

"Well, maybe you're sick. You should go see a doctor."

"No."

"Okay, as you wish. Anyway, do you want to hear the details of how I killed Nine?"

"No. Can we please just eat dinner?"

Eight begins to feel queasy again.

"Sure. But what's wrong? You've always wanted to hear about my murders. Are you sure you're fine?"

Feeling defeated, Eight asks, "Ten, have you ever felt an overwhelming and trembling sensation in your body that makes your head beep?"

Ten looks back at Eight, his eyes wide and fearful.

"You know that's fatal territory you're treading on, right? You know what happens to those who do not suppress their thoughts, right?" Ten whispers, quietly.

"Yes, Ten. I don't need you to remind me."

Eight truly did not need any reminders of what happens to people who experience beeps in their heads. She used to have a friend, Twelve, who lived in the apartment next to hers. Twelve and Eight often hung out when their husbands were at work and even shared their extramarital partners. At the beginning, Twelve made no complaints about her life; instead, she rather enjoyed it.

However, as time passed by, Twelve began to change.

Twelve started to lose interest in infidelity, believing that it was wrong. She then started to behave erratically, often shedding tears when she found her husband with other women and whenever he killed, stole, or lied. Eight has only ever cried when her eyes were irritated, out of physical necessity.

Twelve soon began to complain to Eight about her head beeping. But, Eight paid no heed to Twelve and always disregarded what she said.

Besides, why should she care?

However, one day, while Twelve and Eight were walking around a nearby forest, Twelve began to scream and cry uncontrollably after seeing one stranger kill another, causing everyone around them to stare, confused and cautious.

Twelve made an appeal to Eight, asking her to stop the murder from happening. However, Eight refused to do so.

Why would she do such an unnecessary and silly thing?

Why should she?

After all, murders are such a normal part of human behavior.

Twelve's entire body began to tremble, and her head began to writhe from the torment of nonstop beeping. Despite knowing the consequences, Twelve ran to the crime scene to try and nab the murderer, but before she could reach him, she plummeted to the ground.

Eight watched, with her jaw wide open, as Twelve shattered into a million pieces right before her eyes. Twelve might have been human, but she shattered into pieces as if she was made of glass. Her broken pieces lay, still, on the grassy forest ground. Only a box-like object remained intact, a dark black box with a fluorescent yellow center.

That was the first time Eight had ever seen something like that happen. She always thought it was a rumor that people who become "mentally unfit" disintegrate into pieces, never believing it until she saw it happen with Twelve.

With Twelve's death, Eight constantly has to remind herself that the only way to stay alive is to follow the unspoken rules of Lustville without questioning them.

It was the first time that she had realized that her mind and body are connected. Eight's head continues to beep while she reminisces on this.

Eight desperately wants the images and thoughts of Twelve's death out of her mind, so she tries to distract herself by asking Ten about his day. Ten, always eager to talk about business, begins rambling on about stock markets and trade. However, Eight only ever pretends to be interested for her peace of mind, never truly understanding or knowing any part of her husband's life.

Over the next month or so, Eight tries to forget about the memory of Twelve and the murder of Nine. Usually, forgetting a past lover is easy for Eight as she never lets herself become emotionally attached to her lovers. This time though, the image of Nine's dead body continues to haunt Eight's dreams. However, it is not the thought of missing him that affects her. Rather, it is his gruesome death that plagues her mind every night.

Whenever she thinks about his death, her head throbs, and she begins to tremble uncontrollably.

Fed up with her persistent headaches, Eight soon decides that the best remedy from her headaches is to distract her entire being into her new lover, Eleven. Her relationship with Eleven is passionate, intimate, and drives her sexually insane, but he recently got married and is on his honeymoon overseas. Desperate, Eight looks for a new partner until Eleven returns.

Eight does not usually participate in temporary arrangements. Of course, all her affairs were temporary, but they all lasted for at least six months. Most people usually change affairs after about one month, like Ten does.

Eight could have easily waited for Eleven to come back home to pursue intercourse with him, but she needed to distract her mind from her constant thoughts of morality. So, she decides to call up the one man she knows who would be interested, Thirteen.

Thirteen had expressed an interest in Eight many years back, an interest that he had continued to pursue over the years. Eight is aware of Thirteen's love interest toward her, but she never got together with him because there was always someone better. Thirteen is famous for having very short affairs, the complete opposite of Eight. Now that she is bored, she rings him up to see what he has to offer.

Eight sets up a date with Thirteen for lunch that afternoon at a restaurant that she had picked out. Thirteen was already seated and drinking a glass of Merlot when she arrived. The cozy and quaint restaurant is located in the heart of the busy city, and it is one of Eight's favorite restaurants as it is often known for prostitution.

Seeing Eight, Thirteen jumps up and helps her into her seat. Thirteen is handsome, but Eight had never been particularly attracted to him. He is not that tall, just slightly taller than Eight. He is also lanky, with slender limbs. Thirteen has silver white hair, just like Ten, Nine, and all the other men in town.

Thirteen offers to pour Eight some wine. As he does so, Eight notices blood stains on his fingers but decides to let it go and not question him about it.

"I ordered you your favorite dish. I have been following your BLykeMe feed for years so I know everything about you." Thirteen begins the conversation.

"I don't care. I'm going to get straight to the point. I want us to have an affair." Eight replies.

Hearing this, Thirteen's eyes widen and a smile appears on his face.

"That's amazing!! And perfect timing too! I've been looking for a new affair. My wife is starting to bore me. When do we start?" Thirteen asks, eagerly, jumping up and down like an excited puppy.

"Come over to my apartment tomorrow around noon. I'll be waiting for you." Eight answers, seductively.

The next day, Thirteen shows up, right on time. They watch a movie about killer phones while sitting awkwardly on the sofa, but soon end up in bed, having sexual intercourse at least six times, as expected. Thirteen is a surprisingly good lover, and Eight enjoyed it more than she had predicted. Not once did her thoughts about the past and about Nine's murder pop into her head during her time with him.

Thirteen walks out of her apartment a few hours later, leaving both him and Eight satisfied. Assuming that this was just a one-time affair, Eight expected to never see Thirteen again. She was wrong. She receives a text from him within an hour of him leaving, asking her when he could come back for another round. Reluctant and feeling slightly guilty of what she is doing, she pushes aside her piercing headache, once again, and agrees to see him again.

After a week of sleeping and fooling around with Thirteen, Eight's interest in him begins to deteriorate. Their relationship was fun and different at the beginning because Thirteen was new and exciting, but Eight quickly begins to realize how dull he actually is. Even the sex, which was passionate and lustful at first, became more of a chore than an activity.

However, Thirteen refuses to call it quits on Eight. He wants her, and he refuses to stop pursuing her. He shows up at her apartment even when he is not invited, and he calls and texts her every night, telling her how much he misses her. He gives his full attention to her whenever he is with her.

Thirteen is more attentive to her than any of her previous lovers. Still, Eight is not interested and begins to regret ever asking Thirteen to start an affair, now feeling like she is being stalked.

"I want to end our fling." Eight bluntly tells Thirteen.

"No." Thirteen retorts.

"What do you mean 'no'? I want out. I'm tired of you."

"I mean no. I like you a lot. In fact, I think I love you. I refuse to accept that we are over."

"Love? What? No! Please leave me alone."

"Eight, please. Please, let's continue." By this point, Thirteen's voice has become more high-pitched. He gets down on his knees, begging, with tears flowing down his cheeks.

"Please." Thirteen pleads, while still crying.

Before Eight has a chance to speak, Thirteen's head begins to beep. Memories of Twelve's and Nine's death flood Eight's mind with thoughts of morality once again. The sinking feeling in her stomach returns. Her head begins to throb, and she can hear the beeping noise inside her own head.

Pushing aside her instincts, Eight cannot bear to watch Thirteen shatter the same way that Twelve had shattered. She does not know why, but an urge came over her telling her to intervene. She needs to find a way to help Thirteen before he also disintegrates.

She gets up from the sofa and walks into the kitchen. Thirteen does not follow her. He remains in the same position, on his knees, staring at the silver carpet. Eight searches the kitchen cabinets and finds one of Ten's guns, the same gun he used to kill Nine.

Holding it in her sweaty palm, shaking, Eight walks back into the living room, where Thirteen's head is now beeping faster.

Thirteen sees the gun in Eight's hand and begins to panic, unsure of what she will do but pleading her to stop regardless. His head beeps louder with each plead, and his cries make Eight feel even more uneasy. With one eye closed, she points the gun at Thirteen's head and pulls the trigger. Thirteen falls onto the ground, with his eyes and mouth wide open. His blood splatters onto her long silver dress and stains the carpet.

Eight freezes, unable to move.

'What the hell just happened?' She thinks to herself.

She has never killed anyone before. What came over her? After a minute of shock, she drops the gun and places two fingers on his neck. No pulse. He is dead. She had killed Thirteen.

Eight was expecting to feel calm and relief from killing Thirteen and putting him out of his misery. Instead, she feels a different sensation coursing throughout her body. This sensation is not like the usual; it is much heavier, yet strangely better. She closes her eyes and drifts off as she sits back down onto the sofa, startled by her husband's voice moments later.

"Good God! What have you done?" She hears her husband loudly exclaim.

Eight opens her eyes to find Ten standing over Thirteen's dead body, which has nearly been drained of blood. He bends down and feels around Thirteen's body for a pulse. Nothing. He searches Thirteen, pulls out his wallet and phone, and walks into their bedroom. Eight is now truly a murderer.

Still startled and confused, Eight just wants this feeling of guilt to vanish so she could feel indifferent about everyone around her again. Indifference was all she had ever felt toward anyone and anything. Instead, she feels a rush of sensation overtake her body as she cannot stop shivering.

With a huge grin slapped on his face, Ten quickly returns, whips out his phone, and takes a selfie with Thirteen's carcass.

"I'm so proud of you, and I can't wait to tell everyone in town about it. My wife is a killer, just like me." Ten exclaims to Eight, planting a light kiss on her cheek.

Eight tries to bask in the glory like her husband, but struggles to do so. The sensation continues to overwhelm her. The only solution, she thinks, is to murder all her lovers from this point on in order to make herself stronger and less vulnerable when it comes to death. After all, it is only fair to Thirteen if she does.

Right?

Chapter Five

More than two months have passed since Thirteen's death. Eight no longer loses sleep over him because Eleven is scheduled to return from his honeymoon soon.

Eleven is amazing in every aspect and completely compatible with Eight. Not to mention the fact that Eleven is physically a sight to behold as well. His muscles and abs peek from underneath his silver dress shirt, and Eight always finds herself staring at them.

When they make love, Eight likes to trace his well-defined body with her finger. Eleven has a rugged face and clean-cut and styled silver white hair. He also has the most attractive set of eyes, which shines brighter than the sky beneath the sun.

Their relationship was going well, until it all changed.

One afternoon, Eleven stops by Eight's apartment after work, as usual, to have intercourse with her. However, instead of the pleasurable sensations she is used to experiencing with Eleven, Eight feels a dull, but sharp, pain running through her pelvis and around her hips, which continues to persist even after Eleven leaves.

In attempts to ignore it, Eight grabs a heating pad, places it on her lower abdomen, and switches on the television to watch a fiction movie about a world where everyone is free to have their own individual thoughts. She takes some painkillers and about an hour into the film, she dozes off.

She wakes up to the sound of Ten showering. Eight gets up, hoping the pain had subsided while she was asleep, but the discomfort is still there. She prepares dinner for herself and her husband, and he demands that she has intercourse with him to relieve his stressful day.

Because of an unspoken rule, Eight is not allowed to say no, or both her and Ten will shatter. As he moves in and out of her, the pain worsens, and she begins to bleed, not with blood, but with a black and viscous liquid substance that oozes out of her.

Panicking, she runs to the nearest hospital. By the time she gets there, the pain has become so intense that she falls over and collapses.

Days later, Eight wakes up on a hospital bed, confused as to how she got there. Her doctor explains to her that she has STX, a form of STI that causes her pelvis to devour into itself and liquefy. Eight is shocked.

An STX? Even though STXs are quite common in their society, Eight begins to question how she got one, realizing that one, or multiple, of her partners must have lied about their history. Because almost everyone in town has been infected by STXs, hospitals no longer offer treatment or antibiotics as people have stopped caring.

Eight goes home and finds Ten lying on the sofa, mindlessly clicking through channels. She walks up to him, nervously, and tells him that she has an STX.

However, to her surprise, Ten shrugs it off and continues to stare at the television. Taken aback by his indifference, Eight drops the subject and goes to bed, afraid of starting a fight if she continues to pursue.

The next morning, Eight texts Eleven and asks him to come over. Expecting more sex, Eleven eagerly skips over to her apartment, only to find a stern and angry woman standing at the door.

"Eleven, I have an STX. Why didn't you tell me you're infected?" Eight asks as soon as he steps into her apartment.

"Eight, I don't have an STX. That's disgusting. Why would I tell you about something I don't have? I couldn't have passed it onto you." Eleven replies, looking genuinely confused and irritated that they are arguing instead of having sex.

Seeing the questioning look on Eleven's face, Eight wonders for a moment whether Eleven is telling the truth. However, there is no one else who could have passed it onto her so she continues to press for answers.

"STOP LYING! IT IS YOU!" Eight shouts at Eleven, blowing him back in the process.

"NO, IT'S NOT! STOP ACCUSING ME, YOU FILTHY WHORE!" Eleven shouts back.

Anger and pain flushes through them as both their heads throb. Eight sits down on the sofa to recollect her sanity. So does Eleven.

After several moments of silence, Eight speaks up.

"I'm going to pause our affair until I can figure this out." Eight whispers.

"Fine with me." Eleven sternly replies, as he stands up and silently walks out of her apartment.

Eight continues to sit on the sofa, pondering over Eleven's denial. He didn't seem like he was lying, but people in Lustville are also notorious liars. However, his look of confusion was so genuine that Eight feels herself doubting whether it truly was Eleven who gave her the STX.

Who else could it have been though?

Two days later, Eight receives a text from Eleven, telling her that he is also experiencing symptoms of a STX. He proceeds to imply that it was Eight who passed it onto him, which only stabilized it in Eight's mind that it must have been Eleven who gave it to her, and he's just blaming her for it.

He must have contracted it from his wife or someone else he had recently slept with. Men are always lying to get what they want.

Eight knows that Eleven will not leave her because she has the disease. After all, he has the disease too, and thus, it would be hypocritical of him to leave her for it. She is relieved at the thought of not losing her affair. After Thirteen, Eight is not in the right mood or mindset for another short-lived fling.

Later that night, Eight and Ten begin fooling around when Ten suddenly winces in pain, the same pain that Eight had experienced earlier, and black ooze begins leaking out of him.

Wait a minute. Ten was completely indifferent when Eight first told him about her STX, and now he is liquefying in their bed? Could he have been the one who gave it to her?

"Ten, do you have an STX?" Eight questions him while he is still inside of her.

"What? Of course not." Ten replies, moaning as he answers.

Eight scans Ten's face for the truth as his words no longer mean anything to her. His eyes dart back and forth, and his forehead begins to sweat.

"You're lying." Eight retorts, as she realizes what's happening.

Sighing, Ten finishes inside of her, rolls over onto his side of the bed, and confesses.

"Fine, yes, I have an STX. I am the one who gave it to you. I contracted it when I fooled around with some prostitutes during my business trip last summer."

"What!? Why didn't you tell me?!?" Eight shrieks, sitting up on her side of the bed, unconcerned that her head is beginning to beep again.

"Eh, whatever, it's not a big deal. Now, goodnight." Ten says, ignoring her and quickly falling asleep.

Still baffled, Eight continues to shuffle through her conflicting thoughts. How could he do this to her? How could he not though? Why should he care? Everyone has an STX anyway, so why should it be a big deal?

She can feel her eyes flickering back and forth as she ponders, sparks flying out through her head, and her entire body shaking as though electricity is running through her.

The next morning, Eight hears her doorbell ring as she washes the dishes. She was not expecting company and assumes it's the new neighbors who just moved into her building. To her surprise, she sees Eleven standing there as she opens the door.

"I came here to officially end our affair. I can't deal with all this culpability, and the fact that you gave me an STX and then blamed me for it. I'm done." Eleven speaks, abruptly, as soon as he sees her.

Eight's jaw drops. She is shocked. She never expected an STX to ruin her lust life. She wants to continue seeing Eleven, but she knows better than to disagree with the desires of a man.

"Alright. I understand. But before we officially break it off, can we meet up one last time tomorrow afternoon? Not at my apartment, of course, but at some place else. I'll text you the location."

Eleven nods and leaves.

Eight immediately texts Eleven the location of her favorite restaurant. Eleven telling her that their affair is over triggers beeping inside her head, forcing her to have to resort to her master plan of regaining her strength back.

The next morning, Eight wakes up early to properly reflect on her plan. She moves over to the sofa to avoid waking up her husband, who is sound asleep next to her. She has never committed something like what she is planning before, so she must make sure she has all the details locked and verified.

Ten is slightly surprised when he sees Eight's side of the bed empty after waking up an hour later. He finds Eight on the sofa, but he doesn't say anything to her or question her. He assumes that Eight is still upset about the STX. Not wanting to stir up an argument, he takes a quick shower, puts on his silver dress shirt, and bolts out the front door.

That afternoon, Eight prepares for her meeting with Eleven. She psyches herself up by meditating for two hours and listening to calming music. Is she mentally ready for what she is about to do? Probably not. However, she has no other choice.

She opens her closet door, walks into her wardrobe of dozens upon dozens of long silver dresses. She puts one on, tearing a suggestive slit along one side. She then puts on her finest pair of black pumps and curls her silver white hair into flowing locks. She goes into the kitchen, retrieves Ten's small silver gun from one of the cabinets, and slides it under her garter belt before leaving her apartment.

Eleven is already seated by the time Eight arrives. Seeing Eleven begins to make Eight feel queasy, but she brushes off her thoughts and confidently strides towards him. She then takes the gun out from under her dress and points it at Eleven, whose eyes flare open and jaw drops.

Everyone inside the restaurant stops eating and scrambles to take out their phones so they could post the event on BLykeMe.

Eleven remains glued to his chair, paralyzed. Maybe this is the first time that anybody has ever threatened to kill him. After all, he is relatively young, much younger than Eight.

Eight has never killed anybody in public before. She has only ever killed one person, Thirteen, but that was in the privacy of her own home. She could have easily chosen to kill Eleven privately too, but she needed the publicity. She believes the publicity would make her feel better, stronger, and more invincible.

The past few months had really disconnected her from society, especially with Nine's murder and her recurring thoughts of Twelve. She wants to return to her usual self, back to her reality, back to the flawless and nonchalant author and influencer she is known to be.

Eleven stands up from his seat, so Eight redirects her gun toward him. Before Eleven could move or make a run for his life, Eight shoots Eleven straight onto his forehead, causing him to crumble to the ground the same way that Thirteen did. Blood pours onto the bare restaurant tiles, completely bathing them in crimson red.

More people gather at the scene, coming from afar after having heard the shot. They all cheer and applaud Eight.

After shooting Eleven, Eight feels the same sensation that she had felt when she shot Thirteen rush through her body. The sensation warms her skin and sends shivers through her bones. This time around though, Eight refuses to fall victim to her guilt. She must stand strong.

Perhaps just having that attitude works, as Eight feels the sensation slowly subside. Her head did not ache once. To further cement her place back in society, Eight kneels beside Eleven. She searches for a pulse, but finds none, as expected. Then, with a shaky hand, she takes out her phone from the small clutch she had carried with her.

She opens the camera and forces herself to smile as she poses next to Eleven's dead body, and she snaps a picture.

The crowd continues to cheer, making Eight feel that much stronger.

She posts the photo onto her BLykeMe account and, for the first time in a long time, Eight feels like her old self again, perhaps even better. Maybe she should write a book about her new skill in murdering scorned lovers.

Chapter Six

Ten has always been interested in business, as far as he can remember. Then again, he cannot remember that far back. Ten's earliest recollection of his life is at the age of thirty, just five years back. He cannot remember anything before that time. This used to bother him.

He used to search for answers and clues as to why this is the case until he was warned of the dire consequences he would face if he continued to do so. He had also asked Eight if she could remember her childhood. She could not either, as her earliest recollection is at the age of twenty-five, just five years back also.

In fact, Ten soon discovers that everybody around him only remembers the past five years of their lives.

Five years ago, everyone in Lustville had microchips injected into their brain as part of a psychological experiment, causing them to speak and behave just like everyone around them.

People were no longer able to remember their pasts, their names, or the lives they had before that moment. Because of the chip, if anyone tried to rebel against the commonality of everyone else, the main unspoken rule of the chip, the chip would activate and the person would immediately shatter.

Ten had always worked a normal nine-to-five job as a marketing agent at a small consulting company. People in Lustville were assigned to random jobs when the chips were injected into them. Despite their lives before and the skills they possess, everyone had to completely change their lives and careers.

Men were forced to work menial day-to-day business jobs while women had to become homemakers.

However, men are also given the choice to become entrepreneurs, a given right only men have, if they can make it, that is. A chance to do so came flying at Ten when he married Eight, and for that reason, he likes to call his little enterprise his "wedding gift."

Ten had tried to advertise his idea of a gastronomy food business, where the main source of protein for the meals is the people of Lustville that he murders, to potential investors before, but he was always turned down, forcing him to give up on trying to get funding.

However, the opportunity came up again on the night of his wedding, when he forced his wife to sleep with a potential investor, a rich old man she found repulsive at every sight.

Eight had been aware of Ten's dream of opening his own food chain. However, she didn't have the affair for him. After marrying Ten, Eight realized that marriage didn't mean that she could not continue to sleep around. She only had sex with Ten's investor to ease him into the idea of her having multiple other affairs.

Ten is smart and savvy, so his business grew rapidly over the next three years. However, neither Eight nor Ten expected it to grow as much as it did, and they basked in the wealth that it brought in.

Ten was projected to make his first million by the end of the third year, when the market hit a sudden depression, and the prospect of making his million quickly faded away. However, he was still determined to make it work despite what it took. Who does honest business anyway?

That is how Ten found himself in a meeting with a top tier government official one Tuesday afternoon. It is a rainy day, and Ten could see raindrops hit the large glass window the governor has in his comfortable cabin. Since it is winter, the days are now much shorter. The grey atmosphere outside greatly dims the room inside, which is lit by a single red bulb.

The whole room is mahogany, with wood paneling on the walls and the floor, and wooden furniture encase the entire room. The governor sits behind a large wooden desk, on a black office chair.

The governor is old, far older than Ten. He is pale, and his patchy skin is so thin that Ten can see his chip. The fluorescent yellow center of the chip glistens from beneath his forehead. Despite the cold, perspiration beads shimmer onto the governor's forehead, which he wipes away with a silver handkerchief.

The governor has sunken eyes, a thin mouth, and smells extremely unpleasant. He is dressed in a silver dress shirt and silver tailored pants, just like everybody else, but his garments look more ancient, old, and rusty. No politician ever looks pleasant anyway. The man sits behind a name tag that spells his name, "Zero," while fiddling with his tie.

"So, Ten, I understand that you want me to invest in your business and pull some strings to throw out your competitors?" The governor, Zero, says, in a loud and demeaning voice.

"Yes." Ten replies, frigidly, from his seat in front of Zero.

Zero inspects Ten from head-to-toe, his ugly eyes scanning the length of Ten's body. He wears a look of apathy, which is mainly the only expression that officials are allowed to have.

"Well, Ten, I don't do charity. I would need something from you too."

"What would that be?"

"You see, Ten, I run a successful human trafficking and prostitution business. I don't know if you're aware of that fact or not."

Ten is, but says nothing.

"Luckily for you, I'm letting you help me with this. You see, business has been slow lately. Kidnapping young women is much more difficult now. You know we don't traffic married women. Too much risk for bloodshed, the husbands would pounce on us. Most women are married now, so it has been difficult finding new replacements. If you can get me at least one new woman for my business who is suitable, I will help you with your business." Zero continues.

Ten is not concerned at all about completing this task. Expanding his business is his top priority, so kidnapping a woman so he could have that is not a big issue for him. Plus, he already has someone in mind.

"You have my word. You'll have her soon." Ten replies, standing up.

He gives Zero a firm handshake and exits the cabin with confident steps.

Chapter Seven

Back at his apartment, Ten begins plotting a fool proof plan to kidnap his victim, Fourteen. Ten knows where Fourteen lives, for he had meticulously stalked her for weeks before deciding to murder her husband, Nine, so Ten could marry Fourteen. With his deal with Zero, Ten now has a better plan for her.

Ten had kidnapped Nine one morning while he was still asleep. He had bribed the landlord for a copy of the key to Nine and Fourteen's apartment, and he walked in as soon as he saw Fourteen leave. Ten had created a fake alias to lure Fourteen out of the apartment by pretending to her long-lost sister asking her for help, knowing that she would take the bait as Fourteen always goes out of her way to help others.

Ten drugged Nine, stuffed him inside a sleeping bag, and dragged him to his office. Ten was not willing to sacrifice his precious work hours just for a kill. During lunch, Ten tried to drag Nine back to his apartment so he could kill him. However, Nine woke up suddenly, forcing Ten to kill him on the sidewalk in front of his apartment building instead.

Luckily for Ten, Fourteen would be much easier to lure and capture. She is small and slender, and Ten is confident that he would be able to kidnap her without a threat of challenge. However, despite her size, Fourteen knows that Ten had killed her husband; so, naturally, Fourteen is always cautious when she is around Ten.

Still, how could Ten make sure that Fourteen is the right fit for Zero? What if he spends all this time kidnapping her, and Zero decides to retract his offer to help him? All these thoughts of "what ifs" run through Ten's head, confusing him.

Unable to think clearly, Ten leaves his apartment to go to the local club called "Single Mingles." His last fling had dumped him, so Ten needs another lover to satisfy his desire for infidelity.

While gulping down his fourth shot of Tequila, Ten looks over and sees a young woman sitting down next to him, running her fingers up and down his thighs.

Wanting to grab her by the waist and have his way with her in the bathroom stall, he decides against it so he could save his energy for abducting Fourteen.

Suddenly, a short man comes up to the woman and starts talking to her. Ten gazes at them but remains unaware of what is going on. After five minutes of small talk, the man turns to the bartender for a drink, and the woman walks away. The man then pulls out a packet of mysterious white substance and pours it into the woman's drink, peaking Ten's interest.

She returns, and the man acts nonchalant as if nothing had happened. The bartender also saw what he did but doesn't bother to warn her. Neither does Ten. It was not their place to do so; otherwise, they would be stepping over boundaries, and that is not allowed.

Ten watches as the woman downs her drink and begins to get tipsy almost instantly. Her eyes begin to close, and her body begins to sway back and forth. A few minutes later, the man offers to take the woman home safely and instead, rapes her on top of the pool table and proceeds to lead her out the door.

Raping women is not a sin or a rare occurrence in Lustville. That was not what caught Ten's attention. It was the man's white powder that caught his attention.

Ten has heard about the PCX drug before, but he has never used it or seen it in action. However, now he just might, on Fourteen.

Ten follows the man and woman, hoping to learn more about how to obtain PCX. The man leads the woman into a small room at a shady motel behind the club, completely unaware that he is being followed by Ten.

He locks the door behind him while Ten waits outside, listening to the woman scream in pain, and the man scream in pleasure. An hour later, the man opens the door and finds Ten sitting on the curb.

The man takes one look at Ten, grunts, and proceeds to walk past him.

"Hey, man! Where can I get some of that PCX?" Ten catches the man.

A look of confusion washes over the man's face as he turns around, and then breaks out into a laugh.

"Hold on! Hold on! You mean, you never drugged a woman before?" The man asks, still laughing.

"No, unlike you, I don't need to drug women to get them to go home with me." Ten replies, sarcastically.

"Oh no you didn't just diss me like that! Here, just take this and get out of my sight. I'm sick of you."

Pissed off, the man tosses the small white packet of PCX at Ten and storms off, leaving his one-night stand stranded and unconscious in the room behind him.

Out of lust, Ten walks into the room, where he sees the woman lying on a dirty mattress. Her silver dress is pulled over her head, and her underwear has been thrown onto the floor. After pleasuring himself with the unconscious body, Ten leaves the room and heads home.

The next morning, Ten finds himself in Fourteen's kitchen, spiking her morning pumpkin spice latte with PCX. Fourteen always starts her day off with a pumpkin spice latte, so this would be the perfect trap. Ten hears her walking toward her kitchen so he wedges himself behind her fridge to hide.

Unbeknownst to what Ten had done, Fourteen takes a sip of her latte and immediately collapses onto the kitchen floor. Ten emerges from behind the fridge with thick leather ropes and duct tape, and he ties up Fourteen, throwing her into the trunk of his car while everyone around videotapes them for their live BLykeMe feed.

Almost an hour later, Ten pulls his car up to Zero's cabin and calls him to let him know that he has found Zero's new prostitute. Fourteen is still tipsy and delusional from the PCX, but she has regained enough conscience to the point where she is able to walk.

Fourteen has no idea what she is doing or where she is going, and all Ten could focus on is finally getting his business up and running again.

Ten hustles Fourteen toward the front door, grinning. There is no doorbell, so Ten knocks loudly on the door. After a short wait, a beautiful woman, dressed in full silver lingerie, opens the door and asks Ten what he wants.

"Zero." Ten replies.

The woman's face curves into a seductive smile as she says, "Come in, he's been waiting."

The woman leads Ten and Fourteen up the winding staircase and into the first room on their right. The room is large and expensively decorated. The crimson red and velvet curtains are drawn open, basking the room with bright sunlight. Ten immediately spots Zero lounging, half-naked, on a bed covered with red satin sheets. The woman exits as Zero gets up.

"Well, hello Ten. It's been a while. I thought you had bailed on our plans." Zero says, as he stands up and walks toward Ten.

He pushes Ten aside so he could take a good look at the woman standing behind him. Fourteen sways to and fro, still tipsy, unaware of Zero's presence.

"And I suppose this is the promised young lady? She is a pretty thing. You've done a good job, Ten." Zero applauds.

Zero reaches out a hand toward Fourteen and runs his fingers down her bosom. Fourteen does not flinch at all.

Ten remains silent and still.

"What's her name?" Zero asks.

"Fourteen." Ten replies.

"Well, Ten. You may leave now. I'll get back to you on our deal. First, I need to test her out." Zero says, as he yanks Fourteen's arm and leads her onto his bed.

Ten turns around and walks out the door, confident that Zero would have no issue taking what he wants from Fourteen, as she is still half unconscious.

Chapter Eight

Fourteen wakes up with a massive headache. She finds herself lying, naked, on cold hard marble rather than on her bed and begins to wonder what had happened. She sits up, trying to recollect her thoughts and memories.

Where is she? Fourteen sees her long silver dress hanging on a sad wooden chair, and her memory begins to return. Before she blacked out from drinking her latte yesterday morning, she saw a strange, but familiar, face peeking out at her behind her fridge. Whoever that was must have drugged her.

Fourteen feels lost, exasperated, and frustrated. She is in an unusual place with no idea how she got there. She looks around and observes her surroundings. She sees hundreds of framed photographs featuring naked women, all with blank stares on their faces.

Suddenly, the door flings open. In walks an old man, with heartless eyes and a round belly. Fourteen recognizes who this man is at first glance. This man is Zero.

Fourteen is familiar with Governor Zero and his popular escort business. He traffics young unmarried or widowed women and prostitutes them off to interested men. Nine had always admired the man's business savvy, but Fourteen thinks it's inhumane and disgusting. Of course, nobody ever cares about her opinions. Everyone around her is heartless and cold.

Suddenly, Fourteen begins to register what is happening. She had been trafficked and sold off into Zero's business. Had Zero already violated her? She sniffs, and she can smell his scent on and inside her. Terrified, she backs away from Zero as he reaches his musty old hands toward her.

"Well, someone looks more awake, now doesn't she?" Zero creepily speaks.

Fourteen refuses to answer. Her mind races back and forth, trying to figure out how to escape.

"You're just perfect. I'm so glad Ten brought you to me. I suspect that you will be my top prize and bring my business back to life." Zero grins widely, flashing his rotting teeth at Fourteen.

'Ten?' Fourteen thinks to herself. 'He kills Nine and then sells me off to this creep? What the hell is wrong with that asshole?!'

Zero inches closer toward Fourteen, forcefully gliding his hand down Fourteen's arm. Extremely uncomfortable, Fourteen grabs Zero's arm and throws it away from her. Zero is taken aback, confused, as women are not allowed to deny the desires of men, but proceeds to put his hand on her again.

Then Fourteen remembers. After Nine's death, she started carrying a pocketknife around in her dress to protect herself from potential killers like Ten. How could she have forgotten that? She begins to slowly inch toward her dress, praying that Zero does not notice.

With her heart beating rapidly against her chest, Fourteen concocts a quick plan inside her head to escape Zero. She could smell the stench of alcohol on him, making her want to throw up. She lets Zero caress her arm, hoping it would distract him long enough for her to grab her knife.

Fourteen cringes at the touch of Zero's rough fingers against her bare skin. She had only ever been touched by Nine in Lustville, forgiving Nine while he had his affairs because she knew the chip inside his head caused him to commit acts of sin. She feels nauseous for letting another man, especially an old and bigot one, grope her.

Inching closer toward her dress as Zero continues to stroke her, Fourteen slowly pulls her knife out from her dress without Zero detecting.

She plunges it into Zero's chest, with strength that she didn't even know she has. Struck by the intense pain, Zero falls back, his blood splattering at Fourteen in the process.

Realizing that she had just stabbed someone, guilt begins to overwhelm her as she sprints down the stairs and out the door, still completely naked. She feels relief once outside, able to breathe again, but still panicking at what had just happened.

After several minutes of running, she stops, looks back, and sees Zero's cabin in the far horizon.

Fourteen has no idea where she is. She has no car and no way of getting home. She still could not believe what Ten did to her. Selling her off like that!? How dare he!?

'Ten.' Fourteen thinks to herself. 'What a fraud. How is he married to such a great person like Eight?'

"Eight!!!" Fourteen screams as she suddenly realizes that Eight might be in danger because she's married to a murderer.

Eight was Fourteen's best friend before the whole "apocalypse," as Fourteen likes to call it. They were co-workers, often working on the same projects and cases in a world-renowned scientific laboratory, specializing in neuropsychology and researching how the human mind responds to the depths of modern society.

In fact, everyone in Lustville had actual names before the apocalypse began, only being assigned a number as they enter Lustville. Fourteen's name was Eve while Eight's name was Charlotte. Eve loved Charlotte like her own sister, and Charlotte loved her just the same. At least, until she was taken away by her own invention.

Eve had managed to escape the apocalypse, unharmed, while most others around her weren't so lucky. They no longer remember their pasts, who they were, or even their names, being assigned numbers in place of them to remove the concept of originality.

They had become robots, clones of one another. Eve watched as her loved ones all lost their personalities and memories, one by one.

Eve had to pretend that she was the same as everyone else in order to survive in the new world of Lustville. People in Lustville have no concept of right or wrong, and they have no doubts when it comes to murdering and manipulating others whenever they feel like it.

Eve had to go against her own instincts and join the crowds in cheering and applauding as she witnessed the murder of person after person, feeling helpless and unable to do anything about it. If she didn't join the popular crowd and her chip didn't beep (because she doesn't have one), she would have surely been killed.

Nonetheless, she has to find a way to rescue Charlotte, to bring her back to her senses because she believes Charlotte is the only one who can end the apocalypse.

But how? Like others, Charlotte is also under the control of the chip in her brain. If Eve attempts to remove the chip to stop the brainwashing, Charlotte would shatter into a million pieces. Eve could not bear to even imagine the thought. She would rather Charlotte live as a clone than not live at all.

The sun had risen by the time Eve makes it back into the city, the next morning. The sun is hidden behind heavy rainclouds that fill the sky. The temperature dips low, and the cold breeze touches and kisses Eve from behind.

Freezing because she ran out of the cabin completely naked, Eve dresses herself in disease-filled garments she finds in the woods.

Eve fiddles in her tangled locks for a piece of paper, on which she had written down Charlotte's address years ago and had hidden it in her hair. She glances down at it, barely making sense of what she had written, and begins to walk through the cold and dense forest toward Lustville.

Chapter Nine

Waking up on a cold winter morning, Eight draws open her bedroom curtains to observe the weather. The sky looks grey, laden with heavy rainclouds. There is no sign of the sun, and the temperature drops to below freezing. Eight predicts that the cold will freeze her pipelines so she hurries off to take a shower.

After a quick shower, Eight makes herself a daily breakfast of rice cakes, black coffee, and grapefruit. As a social media influencer, her every step is constantly being watched, and she is not allowed to eat anything else besides what she has been told or else she would shatter.

She sits at the kitchen table, slowly eating her breakfast when the doorbell rings.

"That's strange, who could that be?" Eight says to herself.

Confused and curious, Eight sips her coffee and stands up to open the door, to her surprise.

In front of her stands a woman. A small woman with silver white hair and tangled locks, wearing a torn up and very dirty long silver dress. She smells like she hasn't showered in years, and her pale skin is stained with dried-up blood.

She stands at the door, fidgeting with her hangnail, as she suddenly looks up and sees a woman with the most perfect face and a sharp jawline. She has big doll eyes, with a small scar running down her left cheek.

Upon seeing Eight, the woman's eyes light up in a way that Eight has never seen from anyone before. Her mouth curves into a smile, and her pupils dance. In the woman's expression, Eight observes liveliness and vivacity that she has never seen in anyone else. It is almost as if the woman seems more...human?

Eight has never seen this woman before, but there is something about her face that triggers a recognition in Eight's mind. Eight feels an invisible force surge through her brain and overpower her whole being in a split second.

She cannot understand or identify what's going on, but she feels an unusual sensation creep down from her brain and into the rest of her body, all the way to her fingers and all the way down to her toes.

It is unlike anything she had ever felt before. Sure, Eight frequently feels the power and surge of passion when she is in bed with one of her partners. While that passion felt amazing, it was still much lighter than what Eight is feeling right now. Passion is only skin-deep; this new sensation encompasses her entire being. Before Eight can recognize what is happening to her body, she hears herself say.

"Eve?"

'Eve? Eight thinks to herself as her chip begins to beep. 'Who the hell is Eve?'

"Yes, Charlotte! It's me, Eve." The woman says, cheerfully. "I don't know how you can remember me since you have that chip attached to your brain, but yes, it's me, Charlotte, your friend, Eve."

The woman's eyes warm into a large smile, and she hugs Eight. Eight stands there, at a loss for words and what to do. Who the hell is Charlotte? What is going on? Nobody has ever hugged her like this before. Nobody has ever hugged her at all. She isn't even sure if hugging is allowed in Lustville.

"I don't remember you. I don't know who you are. I don't even know how I know your name, if that's really your name at all." Eight answers, quietly, and motions for Eve to step inside the house.

However, Eve makes no attempt to go inside. Instead, she continues to stand at Eight's front door. Eve has no interest in seeing the inside of Eight and Ten's apartment. She is afraid of what she might find in there since Ten is an infamous murderer.

"Well, Charlotte, you might not remember me, but I was your friend. Your best friend. Your co-worker. Back before this town became a psychological experiment. Back before these chips that you created took over your brains." The woman continues.

Eight still has no idea what this woman is rambling about as her chip continues to sound. What psychological experiment? When was she ever her friend? She doesn't have friends. She never had a job. What co-worker?

Eight cannot remember beyond the last five years of her life. Is this woman lying? Why would she be? How did they know each other? And most importantly, how could she have created these chips when she doesn't even fully understand the power and function of them?

These questions all race through Eight's mind, clouding her sanity. She is still naïve as to who Eve is and what she is talking about.

However, it feels as if her body understands. Her body responds to Eve by making Eight feel strange, but familiar, sensations. Her head continues to beep, albeit quietly and infrequently.

Suddenly, Eve grabs onto Eight's hand. That ensuing moment feels scarily magical. Eight feels an electric shock run through her arm and cloud her mind. Her vision blurs and causes Eight to see a moving picture through her glassy eyes.

In this picture, Eight is sitting inside a laboratory, leaning over a benchtop with Eve. They are both wearing white lab coats with goggles, and are perusing through articles and textbooks while laughing with each other.

"I don't know what you're talking about. What do you want?" Eight says, terrified, as she snaps back into the present and pulls her arm away from Eve.

"You're right. You probably have no idea what I'm talking about, and there's no way to make you remember either. But let me at least try!"

"How?"

"My dear Charlotte, listen to me carefully because I don't have a lot of time. You see, a couple of years ago, you created a chip, a powerful microchip that singlehandedly controlled the minds of the human population. You used to be a psychology professor and an accomplished scientist. You were successful and won many awards for your work on the human mind.

I'm going to give you the condensed version of what happened, and maybe later, I'll fill you in on the details. A decade ago, everyone in Lustville used to be different, with different personalities, statuses, thoughts, and opinions. Everyone had their own voices and their own minds, and they were able to speak and feel as they pleased. However, relentless competition filled the air and war constantly broke out.

People became jealous of each other and wanted to be just like those around them rather than being themselves. This constant obsession with wanting to be the same as everyone else made them suicidal, and they started killing themselves for not being good enough. You observed the human psyche and decided that the emotionally vulnerable could be healed by a device.

So, you created the device, one that would completely take away the feelings and memories of the emotionally vulnerable. It would wipe out their personalities and grant them their wishes of becoming just like everyone else, where no competition or war would ever occur again.

However, the chip only implanted in the brains of those who were emotionally vulnerable, those who secretly craved acceptance and expressed envy for what they did not have, including you, Charlotte. It tried attaching to my brain, but it fell off shortly after.

Well, pretty soon, the chip created this sub-population of people, this society of clones, who lack feelings, morals, and values because everyone is now the same. Your chip took away the uniqueness and personalities that people naturally have in an attempt to save the world.

Because of this, the rest of the world had to create a new planet for people with chips in them, to ensure that everyone would be exactly the same so hate would never occur again, so everyone could feel like they belong in a perfect society, a society where everyone is free to do what they want without consequences, a society where people could murder and cheat, but still have others praise them, a world where everyone can belong.

Unfortunately, the chip did not function as expected, and if anyone decides to have their own thoughts and opinions, if anyone decides to rebel against the commonality of others and tries to have their own morals and voice, the chip would cause that person to shatter into a million pieces.

You created a world where no one is allowed to be different. I don't belong in this world. I live back home, back where we belong, back on Earth. I only pretended like I am part of this world for my husband and for you." Eve faintly lies in attempts to get Eight to believe her, as she grasps Eight's head between her palms.

Usually, Eight would not be bothered by such slander, but part of her body senses a certain truth in Eve, a certain truth that causes her eyes to suddenly shed tears.

Confusion and disbelief overwhelm Eight. What Eve said cannot not be true. Eight could not have been a scientist. Women are not allowed to work. Eve is probably delusional.

"I don't believe you. You're lying. You're crazy! I don't know you. I'm not a scientist or a professor. I didn't create this stupid chip!" Eight retorts in disbelief.

"I understand it's hard, but please believe me, Charlotte. I am telling you the truth. You need to believe. Your husband tried to prostitute me off to Governor Zero AND he killed my husband, and everyone here is STILL applauding him. That's not normal in the world you used to live in! His type of behavior would normally have gotten him thrown into prison for life in the world you came from, the world of social order and morality. This world allows people to commit acts of sin that were not tolerated back on Earth. You don't belong here!" Eve continues.

"Eve, or whoever the hell you are, you have to leave. I don't want to entertain your lies anymore. I have no idea what you're talking about." Eight says, as she tries to close the door. Eve stops her before she is able to do so.

Eve's face is now streaming with tears. Strangely enough, her chip does not beep. Only Eight's chip is beeping. Could Eve be telling the truth? Could it be that she doesn't have the chip?

"Ok, fine. I'm leaving. But, if you ever decide to believe me, which I trust you will in time, please call this number." After saying these words, Eve thrusts a piece of paper into Eight's hand and walks away.

Before Eight could close the door, Eve had wandered off. It almost felt as if she was never here.

Extremely confused by the whole ordeal, Eight locks her apartment door and sits down on her sofa. She hides the piece of paper that Eve had given her inside her dress pocket. Eight continues to ponder on the sensation that she had felt with Eve.

It was not like one that she had ever felt before. It felt different, but exciting. Eight felt separated from her very own mind. It was as if her body recognized who Eve is, but her mind had no recollection.

Ten comes home later that night, and Eight tells him what had happened with Eve. Ten refuses to pay attention to anything Eight has to say after she told him that some girl Ten had tried to prostitute off came to their apartment. He becomes frustrated that he had spent all that time kidnapping Fourteen, just to have her escape from the grasp of Zero. He has to find her or else Zero will take away his investment!

Later that night, after Eight had fallen asleep, Ten crawls out of bed and fumbles through her belongings for any clues as to where Fourteen might be. He had watched her apartment all day but did not see her go home.

Then the phone rings, and it is Zero. Zero tells Ten that he no longer wants Fourteen for his prostitution business, or any woman for that matter, and instead schedules a meeting with Ten to discuss other options.

The next afternoon, Ten finds himself back behind the wooden desk at the musty old cabin of Governor Zero. Zero is fiddling with his tie, as usual, as he speaks.

"Well, Ten, you're not very experienced in the business of trafficking, now are you?"

"No sir, and I'm very sorry." Ten replies.

"After that whole fiasco, I don't want you to traffic any more girls for me. I was almost left for dead with her, and I don't need a repeat of that. However, I have another proposal for you." Zero continues.

"And what's that?"

"Do you know that jewelry store downtown called "The Glam"? It is run by one of my greatest business rivals, who is currently doing better than I am. The shop has an expensive diamond necklace on display, one that is worth half their wealth. Of course, I could just buy it if I wanted to, but why would I want to spend my time and money on that when I can just steal it, right, Ten?"

Ten realizes where this conversation is going. Stealing? That is something he has never done before. Plenty of people did it, but Ten had never been bothered to try it. He found no thrill in it. His heart had only ever been thirsty for bloodshed.

"I need you to steal it for me, Ten. Steal it for me, and I'll invest in your business." Zero demands.

Ten contemplates on it for a minute. Even if stealing is something he has never done before, there is a first for everything. Plus, his business is still his highest priority.

Stealing is something he could easily do if it means his business will thrive, that is, if he plans it out right.

Ten nods in agreement to Zero, and both of them shake hands. Ten then leaves the cabin and begins to plot a fool proof plan to steal the necklace.

Chapter Ten

After that day, Eight had not heard from Eve again. However, Eight still could not get her out of her mind. She sees the outline of Eve's face in her morning coffee, in her mirror as she brushes her hair, and even in her favorite television shows. Sometimes, Eight finds herself staring out the window and seeing Eve's face on the people who walk by.

Eight also continues to have visions of her and Eve, similar to the one she had when Eve showed up days before.

In one of them, she sees herself and Eve drinking coffee at a café that she does not recognize. The café is located outdoors and in the midst of a busy street where everybody has replaced their smiles with frowns toward each other.

Eight sees men and women wearing the most outrageous clothing, different colors and different styles, walking up and down the streets. Both Eight and Eve are laughing and wearing clothes that do not match each other.

Eve is wearing a pink floral dress that reaches down to her knees while Eight is wearing a leather jacket over a white tank top. Everyone looks different. No two people look the same, and Eight can see and hear herself whispering to Eve about how she wishes that she looks like the supermodel on the magazine in front of her.

In another vision, she and Eve are crouching over a mahogany desk, going through some papers that are scattered throughout a welcoming room. They are both wearing the same outfits they had worn in the previous vision.

The whole room is filled with many other desks, over which many other heads are crouching over, with as many men as there are women. Eve whispers something into Eight's ear as her mouth drops open with a gasp when a loud and booming voice interrupts them.

"Densen!" It booms.

The women look, with shocked faces, toward the side of the room the voice had come from.

Suddenly, the vision goes away, and Eight finds herself back on her sofa.

Eight wonders if she should talk to someone, at least a doctor, about the visions that she is having. After all, visions are not normal, right?

However, even doctors would think she's some psycho lunatic if she told them, since being different is not allowed. She would also have to explain to them the constant beeping of her chip, which she is not willing to share with anyone, not even Ten. She knows that if she even mentions her chip, she would instantly become a social outcast and be killed.

Then another vision appears. Eight is sitting behind a small desk, with stacks of books and papers scattered in front of her. Behind her is a tall shelf that towers over her, filled with books upon books on topics related to the psychological mind.

Above her, Eight could see a large banner that read:

"Professor Charlotte Densen on her new book, 'Mind Over Morals'."

In front of her sits a massive crowd of people, both young and old, all dressed in different clothing with different facial expressions, some eager to see her, others arguing with each other, while most bored and staring off into space.

Through the sea of faces, Eight spots a familiar one, Eve, who smiles at her from the front row while holding a sign that reads, "You can do it!" Then Eight hears herself speak:

"Welcome to my book reading. Today, I'm going to read to you a segment from my new book, 'Mind Over Morals'. Thank you for coming, everyone." She says.

She picks up one of the books, which has an image of the brain on the cover, opens it, and clears her throat. Then, she starts reading from it out loud.

"We limit our own freedom. We limit our own free will. How? With a little thing we have come to subconsciously possess, a little thing we like to call 'morals'.

We limit the potential and voice we are capable of by relying on morality. We decide what is right versus what is wrong. We decide who should be punished and who should be rewarded based on our own biased desires and preferences. We create rules that limit some while bringing others to their fruition.

What is morality? Here, I quote an article called the 'Psychology of Morality'. 'Moral principles indicate what is a 'good', 'virtuous', 'just', 'right', or 'ethical' way for humans to behave. Moral rules—and sanctions for those who transgress them—are used by individuals living together in social communities, for instance, to make them refrain from selfish behaviors and to prevent them from lying, cheating, or stealing from others.'

The role of morality is the maintenance of social order, focusing on the display of fairness, empathy, and altruism in face-to-face groups, where individuals all know and depend on each other for survival.

In an analysis provided by Tomasello and Vaish in 2013, this is considered the 'first tier' of morality, where individuals can observe and reciprocate the actions they receive from others, and in turn, elicit and reward cooperative and empathic behaviors that help to protect individual and group survival.

However, there are also abstract moral principles that can be used to regulate and govern the interactions of individuals in more complex societies. This emphasizes more ambiguous concepts such as 'the greater good', leading into what Tomasello and Vaish considered the 'second tier' of morality.

At this level, behavioral guidelines that have lost their immediate survival value in modern societies (such as specific dress codes or dietary restrictions) are seen as essential behaviors that are morally 'right'.

Moral judgments that function to maintain social order in this way rely on behavioral guidelines that were not once seen as important for maintaining order and survival, requiring complex interpretations of moral values and biased judgments.

So, how do we, as a society, deem what is morally right and what is morally wrong? Are we even authorized to determine what morality encompasses based on our own natural discriminations? According to Skitka and Mullen, moral convictions are seen as compelling mandates, indicating what everyone 'ought' to or 'should' do.

Just Like Me
Fallen Victims of the Mind

People are expected to follow these mandates and are emotionally affected and distressed when they don't, and sometimes resort to violence when the values of others do not align with their own. We go back and forth with what we believe should be mandated rules because we want to be able to benefit ourselves and our social groups while casting aside all others. We constantly change our values on what we believe to be important so we can best protect ourselves, even when our actions go against our previous beliefs.

We live in a society where everyone feels obligated to follow social order, with those at the top having more power and control over their behaviors, as well as a stronger voice in altering the concepts of morality at their own discretion, while those at the bottom are more chastised for rebelling against morality and their own social classes. We become envious when we are placed at the bottom of the social chain and are deemed as outcasts.

Those at the bottom are more limited to freedom than those at the top, more limited to what they can or cannot wear, more limited to what they can or cannot say, and more limited to what they can or cannot do.

They resort to rebellion when the values of their free will are shut down by the values of the socially constructed society, creating chaos in the modern world.

However, what if this is no longer the case? What if the rules of social order no longer exist? What if those at the bottom become just like those at the top? What if the world no longer had discriminations and discrepancies?"
Eight stops speaking, and the vision disappears.

Eight is particularly disturbed by this specific vision because of how detailed it was. Her head throbs and aches from it. She goes to bed, despite it still being early, and doesn't bother making dinner for Ten, afraid of how he would react when he found out. Luckily, he does not come home that night.

He has been spending the past few weeks with the new neighbor who just moved into their building while her husband is off on a business trip. She has been constantly messaging Ten about how lonely she feels during the nights when Ten is in bed with Eight, causing Ten to walk out on Eight and straight upstairs.

Over the next few days, Eight does not experience anymore disturbances or visions. The chip had stopped beeping, and she believes that her life is finally getting back to normal. She goes to The Glam and buys herself a new pair of earrings, snapping over thirty selfies of herself in the process.

She spends half her days sleeping with everyone in the local strip club while half her nights drinking and drinking until she could no longer see, believing that shutting off her vision would prevent her visions.

However, then it all returns.

One late afternoon while Eight is washing the dishes from dinner the previous night, she feels another vision blur her eyesight. She quickly sits down on one of the dining table chairs to prevent herself from crumbling onto the ground. She then whirls into another dream like trance, similar to all the ones before.

This time, Eight finds herself having a vision of a chaotic time she is strangely familiar with. The audio begins playing, as she views herself sitting on a strangely colored couch, with the words "I am Charlotte" written across her forehead.

"It has been over 489 days since the outbreak of the mass suicides began, with its first occurrence in Reykjavík, which resulted in over 8,000 deaths, and is continuing to spread like rapid wildfire across several other continents. The death toll is now up to over 100 billion, and it doesn't look like there is an end in sight!

Day after day, citizens of the world are killing themselves due to high insecurity and the pressure of needing to belong. Everywhere we look, people are different from one another. They look different. They behave different. They even speak different! Normal, right? We're human! We're supposed to be different from one another!

Apparently, not!

Unfortunately, little did I personally know, the entire world is filled with normopaths, constantly craving for acceptance and the chance to be like everyone else, and when they don't succeed, bam! They blow up their own brains!

These normopaths cannot handle the pressure that comes with the reality of life, so therefore, the weak continues to off themselves because they fail to match up to the high pressures of social media that literally brainwash them into believing that they HAVE TO BE THE SAME AS EVERYONE ELSE or else their lives are not worth living! Crazy!"

Charlottes grabs the remote control off the wooden coffee table and turns off the news. She had seen enough.

"UGH!!!!" Charlotte grunts, her head burying in between her knees.

"THIS NEEDS TO END! I'm the best scientist in the world! I won over a dozen awards for my work on the human brain! How can I not figure out how to end this madness! I have to end this! I have to do something to stop this!" She screams out loud.

"People are killing themselves by the second just because they are too insecure to have a little confidence in themselves and not listen to the horrid stories of social media, and it's not necessarily their fault! Insecurity doesn't always stem from the weakness and fragility of the mind; sometimes we become insecure because that's how we were raised. Also, who gives social media the right to tell us how we should be living, and that if we don't live the way that they suggest, then our lives are meaningless!? Bullshit!"

"Honey, are you okay? I heard yelling from inside the kitchen." Charlotte turns around and Eight sees an unfamiliar man standing by the kitchen door, holding a spatula from preparing a dinner of roast beef and tomato pasta.

"Yea, sorry, babe. It's the news." Charlotte replies. "It just got to me. It always gets to me. I need some fresh air. I'll be right back."

"Alright, but be careful out there! People these days do not know what they want. I almost got my arm bit off and returned to me on my way home from the grocery store earlier!"

Frustrated and stressed out, Charlotte walks out of her home and heads off toward the direction of the bridge, mumbling to herself and fidgeting with her fingers as she continues to walk straight. On her way there, she encounters more suicides in person than she had just seen on TV moments ago.

"Jesus, this is really getting out of control." Charlotte whispers to herself.

Over on her left, she sees five cars speeding toward each other and colliding, with all eight people flying out through their windshields and onto the hoods of the opposing car seconds after. Over on her right, she sees people shooting themselves in the heads after reading comments from trolls on social media and losing followers.

Behind her, she can hear more guns firing and ambulances whirling as they are unable to get to the injured because of the chaos that the town has created.

Charlotte then feels her pocket vibrate. Someone had commented on her latest social media post, where she posted a picture of her and her friends celebrating her birthday at a café. The newest comment says, "Charlotte, maybe you should hit the gym instead of the bakery! I think you're done stocking up on rolls."

Her heart and stomach sank. Charlotte's weight was always her biggest source of insecurity. She always fears that with enough comments like these, she may one day end up killing herself also.

"How could people be so cruel? Why can't it just be okay that I don't look like a supermodel in every photo? Why can't it just be okay that I don't look like a supermodel at all?" Charlotte groans in anger and frustration.

Still, despite her opinionated thoughts and strong feminism, her insecurity continues to creep through. She covers her abdomen with her long cardigan and continues walking. She watches as more and more people jump off the bridge as she crosses it.

She used to intervene when she sees jumpers. She used to try and talk them down, and a fraction of the time, she was successful. However, now it has gotten to the point where there are too many of them to control, and it's better to just leave it.

Charlotte continues to walk until she sees a petite lavender colored home.

"I still can't believe she went with that ugly color. How could she not care what people think of her?" Charlotte says to herself.

She knocks on the door. A woman opens it and smiles.

"Eve, we need to talk." Charlotte demands, as she shuts the purple door behind her.

Chapter Eleven

Weeks had passed by, without any news from Eight. Eve did not expect Eight to suddenly believe her and reach out to her, but somewhere in her heart, she had hoped that she would.

Over the past few weeks, Eve had isolated herself inside a small cottage on the outskirts of town to avoid being found. With Nine dead and the assumption that Ten is still on the hunt for her, she no longer feels safe in her own home. She does not trust the people of this society; lying is in their blood.

Eve had stumbled upon this old cottage a few years back, expecting that one day she would need it if her life is ever in danger.

Eve knows in her heart that the only hope to save the people of Lustville is to revive the creator of the chip, Eight, to get her to reverse the effects, and the only way to do that is to kidnap Eight and force her to remember, force her to remember why she began the invention, force her to remember the research she began working on to stop it.

One gloomy morning, Eve, with the help of a professional kidnapper, sneak into Eight's apartment, drug, and blindfold her as she comes out from the shower. They then load Eight onto the back seat of Eve's car and drive her off to an abandoned building with an office where Eve has been stashing all of Eight's old research.

Eve parks her car across the street from The Glam, places Eight's arm over her shoulder, and drags her into the building and up a dusty and crooked staircase. She hears sirens blaring, cameras clicking, and people applauding behind her but does not care enough to turn her head around to see what's going on.

Eve opens the door of the office and leads Eight inside. With her eyes now slightly open, Eight sees a room with boxes upon boxes of old documents scattered across the floor.

Fearful that Eight might escape, Eve quickly locks the door and shoves the key into her bra. She pushes Eight into the seat behind the desk, rummages through one of the boxes, and takes out a pink folder filled with papers.

"Here, read this." Eve says, as she tosses the folder in front of Eight.

Eight opens the folder and finds an article she had presented eight years ago on the concept of "Normopathy," titled "Who Are You Really?" She picks it up and begins reading.

Have you ever wanted to be like someone else, where the need becomes so strong that you continue to obsess over that desire, refusing to stop until you have achieved that goal? Have you ever despised the body you are in because it doesn't 'align' with the common body type of those around you? Have you ever pursued to belong and pursued for acceptance so intensely that you lose yourself in the process?

'Normopathy' refers to when an individual person, or a group of people, strive to conform and be accepted by the greater society, even if it means risking the loss of their own individualities. Normopathy can also refer to the desire to relinquish individuality because it creates a sense of 'difference' and 'not belonging'.

During the 1970s, a psychoanalyst, Christopher Bollas, termed the phrase 'normotic illness', where people resort to mental breakdowns and violence in response to not fitting in. People who suffer from normotic illness fear loneliness. They always feel the need to belong and yearn for social approval.

'Normopaths', as they are called, lack their own opinions and thoughts. They refuse to act or speak unless they are told to or unless they are certain that their thoughts and opinions will align with that of others. They constantly fear rejection so they look to others on how to behave. These people form their likes and dislikes based on popular opinions, never wearing an outfit before someone else has worn it first and never reading a book before someone else has read it first.

People with normopathy have developed this 'illness' as a source of security. They have had traumatic pasts, either in childhood or young adulthood, where their voices and beliefs have been constantly met with dissatisfaction, criticism, and anger. They have been constantly told they are 'wrong' or that they exist to create chaos and havoc rather than exist for the greater good of humanity.

These people are usually timid and shy, refusing to speak up in crowds except for when they have been addressed directly, and even so, only speak up in agreement. They are met with extreme guilt and shame when they find out that they have disagreed with the larger crowd, only fueling their silences that much more.

Normopaths no longer know why they feel certain ways, only knowing that they should because everyone else seems to. They no longer behave as functional human beings. Rather, they begin to exist as objects that simply agree and nothing else. They feel empty, unable to generate self-acceptance so they seek external validation.

Every day, we are surrounded by normopaths, unable to tease them out from the crowd because they are experts at fitting in. Our minds are trained to identify and perceive the outspoken and loud as 'being different' rather than those who go unnoticed. Normopaths are the people who want to be like us, as well as the people we want around us, creating a double-edge sword.

Chapter Twelve

Eight stops reading midway through the article, lights a match, and burns the papers. She cannot believe the useless and manipulative knowledge that lied inside that article.

'An obsession to be like everyone else? Preposterous!' Eight thinks to herself.

As someone who has become increasingly popular and famous for her writings on individualism and self-acceptance, she refuses to believe that there are people who would want anything but that.

Eve kept Eight locked in the room for many days on end. Throughout these days, all Eight is able to do is read and read piles of articles. She does not attempt to escape, even though she is much stronger than Eve and can if she wants to. She finds herself drawn into her readings, and slowly by slowly, she begins to remember her past.

Eve gradually begins to fill Eight in on what had happened. Eight learns that she had created the chip with the intention of solving the psychological issues of the emotionally vulnerable, to prevent further suicidal behaviors, and to attempt to give people their sense of free will back.

She had intended to make the weak stronger and to devoid the rich and powerful of their excuses to dehumanize the lower class. She had intended to also solve the chaos caused by the clashing of opinions.

Eight remembers now how people argued and fought due to differences of opinions and beliefs between social groups.

In attempts to resolve this, she created a chip that causes everyone's brain and consciousness to become EXACTLY the same, to remove the modern differences of morality and appearances, to remove conflicting thoughts and opinions, to remove the social order and make the behaviors of everyone the same, to remove the concept of restrictions and limitations and allow everyone to have free reign, to utilize the full potential of individual thoughts and preferences, and to completely remove the consequences associated with going against the moral guidelines constructed by society.

She had intended to cure diseases such as depression and jealousy, that created acts of violence. She wanted to ultimately remove the chaos in the world that had caused people to become suicidal for not measuring up to those at the top of the ladder chain and for not measuring up to the impossible standards of society.

However, her research had been highly subjective and discriminatory when it should have been more objective and factual. She failed to take into account that the mind functions in conjunction with the physical body, unable to alter one without affecting the other.

The chip had been a carefully researched device with great promise and potential but ended up becoming a poor and disastrous invention. It had deprived humans of their humanity and only latched onto the minds of the emotionally weak, turning them into clones of one another with pre-programmed emotions, engaging in behaviors without understanding the consequences, instead of emotionally strong humans with self-acceptance and self-love.

It created a society of murderers, liars, cheaters, and all things sin rather than a society of equality and social justice.

As Eight learns more about the chip, she no longer feels trapped and confused. She now begins to understand the reason for her apathy and self-destructive behaviors, and why she had felt conflicting thoughts but had no control over them.

The more Eight recollects her studies and work, the more determined and engaged she becomes in continuing her research on how to undo the apocalypse created by the chip. She finds herself becoming more emotional to her memories of murdering and cheating as she learns to become more human.

However, as Eight's emotions become more developed, she suddenly finds herself becoming more depressed. She finds herself becoming more disappointed over issues she would not have normally been disappointed over, such as her husband's disregard for her absence, and his continual infidelity, actions she believes are results of the brainwashing. Ten has not called Eight once, but instead, had posted about his newest affair on BLykeMe.

Eight's visions do not stop, but they make much more sense to her now. She soon begins remembering bits and pieces of her old life, such as how she likes to eat bacon and eggs for breakfast rather than plain rice cakes, how she used to be loyal and devoted to her boyfriend who still lives back on Earth, how the thought of infidelity and being with Ten disgusts her, and how she used to be a strong and independent woman, with an outspoken mind, rather than a submissive whore.

Eight then finds a video, a DVD of a recording from when she presented her research on the chip at an annual scientific conference in Osaka. She inserts it into the outdated DVD player beside her and begins watching.

"The human mind is very complex. It is both intellectual, yet dysfunctional, and when steered in the wrong direction, it can wreak havoc on society. The social order of society has taken away the human right to choose and belong, forcing us to fight for what is ours and fight for our place in this world, putting a dent in the structure of order and as a result, creating even more destruction, and sometimes even death.

Look around you. Everyone wishes they could be someone else. The wealthy wishes to achieve more humility and compassion. The humble wishes to achieve more materialism and success. Not one single person around you is satisfied with his or her life.

People wish that they can be the person on their right or the person on their left, creating a mindset of social dysfunction and depression. Over the past sixteen months, nearly 100 billion people have committed suicide because they wished to be different, to be someone they were not, and when they did not fulfill that need to fruition, they lost hope in living.

You are sitting in this auditorium today because you wish you could also be different. You wish you could be the person sitting next to you, be the person who fits in with society, and be the person who no longer have to follow the social order of structure. You are tired of the constant limitations that confine you to your part of the world, unable to interact with those from other parts, and unable to enact in the behaviors and mindsets that those in other groups are able to.

Well, ladies and gentlemen, you no longer have to live in a world of anger and envy. You no longer have to live in a mindset where you constantly yearn to be someone else or constantly yearn to be able to engage in the activities and behaviors of those in other social groups. You no longer have to utter the words 'That's not fair' to yourself.

I present to you 'Separvoc', the first genetically designed microchip that grants your wishes to become just like everyone else. No longer will you have to live in the anxiety and envy of being different. No longer will you have to scroll through the social media pages of influencers and wish you are them instead of yourself. No longer will you have to be an outcast in a world where the upper class have different rules than the lower. No longer will you have to subject yourself to restrictions, where you are unable to express your own voice and opinions.

With Separvoc, everyone becomes the same, everyone is given equal chance to speak and behave as they wish without the rules of the social order imposed on them. Envy will cease to exist because differences will become a thing of the past.

Imagine a world that is a complete replicate of the one you have always dreamt of, a world where you are free to express your emotions and desires without the morals of society limiting you to certain actions and phrases. A world where the concept of free will can truly exist. Imagine a world where anything and everything you want become reality, a world where violence and suicide have vanished, a world where everyone can be satisfied and happy.

Separvoc detaches your mind from your body, allowing you to behave without the constant thoughts and worries of guilt and shame that would otherwise prevent you. Your mind no longer prevents the desires of your body from coming to life. Your mind is no longer controlled and limited from expressing the life your body wants to express.

Separvoc is designed to attach to your brain, making you believe that morals no longer have to be followed and differences are no longer a part of reality. Separvoc is the invention of the future, where everyone becomes one, and no one will ever need to suffer again."

Chapter Thirteen

Eight finds herself growing increasingly depressed and conflicted over the next few days, as she battles between the powers of the chip and her own personal instincts. The chip in her head beeps louder and louder the more Eight learns about her past and tries to deactivate Separvoc.

The more she learns about the new world she has created, the more increasingly aware she becomes of the people around her. She begins to notice how similar everyone is and how robotic everyone has become.

Everywhere she turns, people are walking down the streets, with simultaneous steps one by one, smiling endlessly without reason on blank faces, and posting updates and photos on their phones regardless of where they are.

Everyone around Eight looks exactly the same, the only difference being the gender. Men and women both have silver white locks on their heads while adorning their bodies with silver garments and black shoes.

However, the strangest part is, no one seems to notice. The people do not seem to be aware of the fact that they look exactly like the people walking on either side of them. The people of Lustville do not seem to be aware that they post their outfits on BLykeMe, thinking they stand out, when only one outfit exists in the entire town.

The chip makes Eight want to conform to the heinous rules that her current society follows.

It wants her to shut down her feelings and morals. Although Eight could have done that previously, her learned knowledge causes her to feel extreme guilt for creating the apocalypse that destroyed society and resulted in the deaths of so many people when she was only trying to save them.

The final straw came one afternoon. Tired with her reading, her mind saturated and foggy, Eight walks down the street to grab a cup of coffee from the local café. On her way there, she hears a woman scream loudly behind her. She turns around and sees a young girl being stabbed multiple times by an older man after she was mugged and raped.

Eight watches as the girl bleeds to her death on the hood of a rusty car while everyone, even the police, around her continues to take pictures, not one single person caring enough to call an ambulance. She then walks over and leans closer. It was Eve. She had been attacked while running out to her car to grab the files that documented how Eight could turn Separvoc off.

Usually, Eight would not have cared. In fact, she would have joined them in snapping photos, even taking a selfie with the body to boost her social media pages. However, this time, she could not shake what had happened.

Over the course of the past few weeks, she had developed morals and emotions that now cannot be distracted with anything else, not even lust. She had attempted to sleep with every man she saw walk down the streets, but her mind refused to let her proceed past first base as she began to feel guilty for potentially cheating on Ten.

Eight's head throbs, her vision blackens, and she could feel sparks of electricity shooting out from the top of her head. Her entire life begins to flash rapidly through her mind as she experiences her entire timeline, from childhood to when she first became interested in the human mind to her first job to her first relationship, all within seconds.

Separvoc is glitching and malfunctioning because Eight has broken the unspoken rules of having morals and emotions, for caring about the feelings of others, and for experiencing guilt for her actions of free will.

She can no longer bear the pain that her head is causing her. She knows too much to distract her mind and turn the chip off, and she never got the chance to read up on how to deactivate it. Her only option now, is to cut the chip out, to remove it before it causes her to shatter and disintegrate.

The pain increases, and Eight runs like a lunatic through the streets of Lustville, screaming to herself to stop the agony, while everyone in town watches in confusion, distraught, and fear.

Eight makes her way to an isolated river in the secluded forest, takes a knife out from under her long silver dress, flowing in the wind, and makes a deep cut into her right temple, digging her fist into her head, laughing insanely, as she rips out the electrified microchip and drops it in the water.

"I want to be just like everyone else. I want to be just like everyone else. I want to be just like everyone else." Eight says, repeatedly, laughing as she steps into the river, falls back, and flows away with the current, leaving a trail of blood behind.

The entire town of Lustville had gone to the river, hoping to witness and record the downfall of the town's "lunatic." However, rather than taking out their phones, like they used to, one by one, they each pull out their own knives and cut into their own right temples, one by one, reaching their fists inside their heads and pulling out their own individual microchips.

They do not know why, but watching Eight do it compelled them to also do the same. One by one, each person drops their electrified chip onto the muddy ground, stomps on it, and one by one, they each walk into the river, fall back, and wash away with the current, leaving a trail of blood behind in the dark, cold, empty, and silent town of Lustville.

Epilogue

Differences in human personality serve as a way for us to express our own individualities and strive to become the people we want to be. We were all born different, all born with different thoughts and opinions on morality and how we should function as part of society.

The social order of society was created to prevent those with mindsets of harming themselves and others from coming to fruition while allowing those with mindsets of achieving the greater good to flourish.

We think we want to be the same as the person next to us. We think that if we are just richer, prettier, or smarter, then our lives would be better. We look at influencers, celebrities, and supermodels, wishing we have their lives.

But envy is only temporary. We think we know what we want because our current lives are going downhill while it seems like the lives of others are only getting better and better.

However, what we don't realize is that each and every person has their own strengths and weaknesses. Having what everyone else has or being what everyone else is removes our own individualities, causing us to become numb and robotic creatures who blindly act and speak without knowing why.

A world where everyone is the same only welcomes chaos and destruction. We think we cannot be happy with our individual differences, but a world that takes away uniqueness and order only leaves us craving for more.

We are all different for a reason, to share with others what they do not have while receiving what we do not have. Not everyone's appearance represents how they truly feel on the inside. Becoming someone we wish we could be cannot solve our problems.

Being on the opposing end of the social construct doesn't always guarantee satisfaction. Running away from our difficulties is never the answer.

We are most vulnerable to change and ideas when we are emotional. Our emotions are what make us unique, yet they are also what drive us toward change and dissatisfaction. We have the tendency to not disagree with those around us for the fear of becoming social outcasts. We have the tendency to become who and what others want us to be even when we disagree.

Just Like Me
Fallen Victims of the Mind

Be careful for what you wish for.
You might just get it.

Just Like Me
Fallen Victims of the Mind

Based on true experiences of the modern world.

Just Like Me
Fallen Victims of the Mind

Just Like Me
Fallen Victims of the Mind

Just Like Me
Fallen Victims of the Mind

www.ingramcontent.com/pod-product-compliance
Lightning Source LLC
Chambersburg PA
CBHW021204110726
47900CB00002B/729